MISTER Tonight

KENDALL RYAN

Content Editing by

Elaine York and Becca Mysoor

Copy Editing and Formatting by

Pam Berehulke

Cover Design by

Uplifting Designs

About the Book

Last night was the most embarrassing night of my life.

I was *that* girl.

You know, the highly intoxicated chick celebrating her thirtieth birthday with her two best friends—who are happily married. And the more I drank, the more I wanted to do something reckless to celebrate.

By reckless, I mean the sexy and alluring man dressed in a business suit standing near the bar. You know his type—tall, dark, handsome. I was sure he was out of my league, but I'd had just enough alcohol that things like that no longer seemed to matter. I'm not fat, mind you, but you can tell I like french fries, so there's that.

He took me home, and I enjoyed the hottest birthday sex of my life. Well, until it came to a screeching and rather unwelcome halt.

There's nothing quite like being interrupted mid-ride with a little voice asking, "What are you doing to my daddy?"

Just kill me now . . . or so I thought.

Come to find out, the man I rode like a bull at the rodeo is my new landlord.

Chapter One

Kate

"I need to get laid tonight."

Jessie laughed while Rebecca handed out a round of tequila shots.

I tossed back the shot, screwed my face up, and stuck my tongue out, trying not to cough. "It's so bad," I said on a groan, the liquor burning my throat.

"Here." Jessie shoved a lime wedge into my mouth.

After our second (or was it the third?) round of tequila shots, I had pretty much confirmed that I was no better at downing them now than I had been in college. And yes, I knew that I was probably too old to drink tequila shots, but I was determined to reclaim part of my youth with my two best friends before I officially turned thirty at midnight.

"Happy birthday, Kate," Rebecca said, handing me a Corona this time.

"Cheers to being thirty." Jessie grinned as we clinked bottles.

"Thirty and homeless," I added, taking a large swig.

Jessie shook her head. "You're not homeless. You just . . . don't have anywhere to live."

Rebecca and I laughed, used to her constant optimism.

My roommate had just gotten engaged, and a couple of weeks ago she'd sat me down to tell me I was being evicted. My stomach sank as I thought about our conversation. Apparently, she and her new fiancé didn't want me third-wheeling all the time. Which was understandable, but it didn't make me any less upset to have to move out of my rent-controlled apartment that was just down the street from my favorite coffee shop *and* frozen yogurt shop. You know what they say . . . *Location. Location. Location.*

"How's the search?" Rebecca asked, shoving a lime wedge into her beer.

"I put a deposit down on an apartment this week," I said, taking a swig. "I just need to go look at it tomorrow and make sure the landlord isn't a psychopath."

I'd found the apartment through an online ad. It seemed promising, spacious with lots of light and a nice little nook where I could set up an office. I wrote a successful weekly gossip column, and since I worked from home, a comfortable place to write was an important part of my living space.

"Enough adult stuff." Jessie put her arm around my shoulders. "We're here to celebrate."

"One more beer and I'll officially be drunk," Rebecca said, scanning the bar. "Which means we should find you a guy now before the beer goggles set in."

Rebecca, Jessie, and I had all been roommates in college. Jessie was a serial monogamist who had gotten married when we were twenty-four, and Rebecca had married her long-term boyfriend last year. Ever since they'd said *I do*, they'd tried to set me up with basically every available guy in a fifty-mile radius.

I didn't mind the setups as long as the guy wasn't expecting to get into something serious. I liked my life the way it was and lived by my personal motto: *Don't mess with a good thing.* Besides, after watching my sister go through a very messy divorce with the man who was supposed to be the love of her life, I wasn't exactly in a rush to settle down.

I looked around the bar. There were plenty of guys, but nobody who excited me. I needed to find someone who was looking for the same thing as me. Fun, casual sex. No strings attached.

I was on the verge of giving up when I saw *him*.

My breath caught in my throat, and my heart did a little jump for joy. He was leaning against the bar, casually sipping a beer. He looked like he was in his late thirties, and trust me when I say he was the total package. Tall with short, dark hair and a killer smile. He wore a perfectly tailored suit, like he'd just come from the office. I was a huge sucker for a guy in a nice suit, and based on the way it fit, I had a feeling he'd look even better without it on.

He laughed, revealing a perfect jawline and cheekbones that belonged on a *GQ* cover model. I swallowed, a little shiver running down my spine as I imagined him wrapping those firm biceps around me.

He was the hottest man I'd ever seen, and he looked like he'd fit in better on the cover of a magazine than he did drinking a Heineken in a bar called Bucky's. I bit my lip, unable to stop myself from imagining climbing on top of him and celebrating my birthday by riding his . . .

"Kate, hello."

Rebecca waved a hand in front of my face. I'd been practically drooling over Mister Perfect, totally forgetting that my friends were there.

"Sorry." I laughed, nudging my head in his direction. "I think I found my Mister Tonight. But don't look at the same t—"

Before I could get that sentence out, both Jessie and Rebecca were craning their necks to get a look at him. I mentally slapped my palm on my forehead, hoping he hadn't noticed them staring right at him.

"Oh, he's hot," Rebecca whispered, turning back. "And he has this *thing* about him."

She was right. He had a vibe, a raw sexual appeal that practically pulsed in the air between us.

"If that *thing* is a large bulge in his pants, then yes," Jessie added.

Rebecca nodded. "Well, he is really tall. I'm thinking *things* might be proportional."

"I think he just smiled at us," Jessie said, grinning.

I sneaked a quick glance. He was definitely looking in our direction. *Shit.* "Is he out of my league?"

"You're gorgeous," Rebecca said earnestly. "He'd be lucky to date you."

I shook my head. "Not date. Just birthday sex. I'm looking for a Mister Tonight, not a Mister Forever."

"But seriously, look at him. *Fuck.* The things I would do to him if I wasn't married . . ." Jessie bit her lip.

"Exactly. He's like a twelve out of ten. And I'm . . ." I looked down at my outfit, a black cocktail dress that only barely concealed my curves.

I wasn't fat; I was pleasantly plump. Curvy. Ample. Sturdy, if you will. But yeah, you could tell I liked french fries. And that I liked to dip those fries in ranch dressing.

Rebecca pressed her hand on the small of my back, nudging me out of my introspection. "You're a total babe."

"Just go over there and say hi," Jessie said, taking my empty beer and giving me a little shove.

Normally, I'd be too shy to approach a guy that jaw-droppingly handsome, but the last tequila shot we'd taken had apparently obliterated all my common sense, as well as my verbal filter. It was my birthday, and I'd be damned if I didn't at least get a hot make-out session. I hadn't shaved my legs and squeezed my butt into a too-tight dress for nothing.

I gave myself a mini pep talk and was ready to walk over to him when I realized he wasn't there anymore. *Fuck*. Had I missed my chance?

My heart sank.

"Excuse me," a deep voice said from behind me.

I turned and felt myself flush. He was standing there, all six-plus feet of him, and he was smiling. At me.

"I'm Hunter," he said, holding out a hand. "I figured

instead of trying to make eye contact through a crowd of people, I should just introduce myself."

He was sexy, funny, and straightforward? I was in full swoon.

I slid my hand into his. "I'm Kate."

Not one to be shy, I looked straight into his warm brown eyes, electricity running through my body from his touch. He had big, strong hands and a firm grip. I was having a hard time shaking off the image of what those big hands could do when I realized he was speaking to me.

"Can I get you a drink?"

"Of course." I smiled seductively, almost not believing it was working out so well. I must have had some majorly good karma to land this guy.

Before he turned to order, his gaze slid over my curves, taking in my little black dress that left very little to the imagination. *Did they turn off the air-conditioning?* Heat rushed from my cheeks down to my chest and settled between my legs.

"What are you drinking?" he asked. His full lips and movie-star smile made everything he said sound dirty.

"Whatever's fine," I said, trying to keep my cool. "Just not tequila."

"I noticed you taking a shot earlier. I don't think I've ever seen someone make a face like that before." He smirked, and I put my hand on my hip in mock offense.

"Are you always this complimentary to women you meet at bars?"

"I guess that's the reason why I'm still single." He grinned, signaling to the bartender.

I laughed, wondering how it was possible that this guy *was* single.

After a minute, he turned back with two martinis. "So, what's the occasion?" He held up his glass in a toast.

"It's my thirtieth birthday," I said, clinking my glass against his and taking a sip.

"Happy birthday. So, how does it feel to be thirty?"

"I'll let you know at midnight." I grinned, looking

him up and down. "But I have a feeling it's going to feel pretty damn amazing."

Jesus, Kate. This was why I shouldn't drink tequila. I lost all my inhibitions.

I was afraid I'd come off too strong, but Hunter didn't seem to mind. He was watching me closely with a sexy, deep stare, his gaze occasionally dropping to my lips as he spoke.

What had he just asked me? Oh yeah, he'd asked if I had any interesting hobbies.

I sucked in a breath and smiled. "Yes, actually, I love to cook."

"What a coincidence. I love to eat."

Chuckling, I shook my head. "You do understand your pickup lines are awful, right?"

He grinned at me, an amazing, mega-white smile that said he was both amused by me and not the least bit bothered that I was poking fun at him.

"I'm actually glad we bumped into each other tonight. I mean, your game needs a lot of work," I added.

"And you're offering to help?" His eyes crinkled at the corners.

I pursed my lips, looking him over. "Depends. What's in it for me?"

"The satisfaction of knowing I won't be out there somewhere inflicting horrible pickup lines on some unsuspecting girl?"

I shrugged. "Fair enough."

He took another sip of his drink, watching me over the rim of the glass. "Where do we begin?"

I tapped my finger against the side of my glass, appraising him coolly. "You're going to need a lot of work."

His mouth twitched in amusement. "Clearly."

After setting my glass on the bar, I turned to fully face him. It was like being smacked across the face with a *GQ* magazine.

I swallowed. "Let's start with . . ." My gaze locked mischievously on his. "What's really on your mind right now?"

Hunter didn't answer right away. His gaze dipped again, ghosting over my cleavage and then my lips before returning slowly to my eyes. "I want to know how a woman like you could possibly still be single at thirty. And I want to know if you taste as sweet as you look."

My cheeks grew warm. Okay, then. Maybe he did have some game.

"Is that all?" I asked, slightly breathless.

"I want to know the noises you make in bed. And other really inappropriate things you're not supposed to talk about the first time you meet someone."

"I see," was all I could manage.

Hunter leaned a little closer, our knees touching beneath the bar. "Does that let you know where my head's at right now, and which areas I'll need the most help with?"

You could practically cut through the attraction buzzing between us with a knife. It was definitely too warm in here, and my insides felt all melty. In a good way, not in the *I'm going to toss my cookies* kind of way.

"Very much so." I took another sip of my drink before returning it to the bar. Time to move to a safer topic. "So, the martinis, the suit." I gestured at his outfit, trying to keep my mind on the conversation and off of Hunter's package. "Are you some kind of high-powered businessman?"

"Not exactly." He gave another low, sexy laugh, rubbing a hand on the back of his neck. "I'm a civil engineer for the city. You know, building projects and public transit. Really exciting stuff," he added sarcastically.

I smiled, relieved he wasn't a business exec. I'd slept with enough of those to last a lifetime. Dry and boring, and about as exciting as a baked potato. "No, I think it's great."

"Most women tune me out as soon as I say *public transit.*"

"Well, I'm not most women," I said with a smirk, looking into his eyes again.

"I can see that." He held my gaze for a moment before taking another sip of his martini.

Normally, I was so confident and relaxed, but this

man . . . he was on a whole other level of sexy.

"I have to admit," he said as he leaned in closer, "I just ordered the martinis to impress you. I'm usually a beer guy."

I tried to keep my jaw from dropping. *He* was trying to impress *me*? I hadn't expected that.

"So, what do you do?" he asked, interrupting my thoughts.

"I write a gossip column."

Usually, guys shut down when I say that, thinking it was a fluff job or a hobby. But Hunter nodded with interest, listening to my every word. And the sexual tension between us was crackling like a low fire, just waiting to be stoked back to life again.

"That's way more interesting than my job. How did you get into that?"

I shrugged. "I've always loved writing. I didn't necessarily picture myself writing about celebrities, but a friend of mine had an in for this job, and I was sort of a natural, so I kept doing it."

"That sounds fun."

"You'd be surprised." I set my empty glass on the bar. "It's a lot of sitting alone in my apartment in sweatpants, researching stories. But don't get me wrong, I love what I do."

The conversation flowed easily between us, and as we sat there talking and flirting and laughing for another hour, I realized I hadn't had this much fun in a long time. His eyes were a hypnotic shade somewhere between coffee and cognac, and it was refreshing to talk to a man who was so easygoing and who actually seemed to be interested in what I had to say and not what I could *do* for him. This much of a connection really wasn't necessary, as I was only looking for a good time, not a lifetime partner. But still, it was nice.

He finished the last of his martini. "Should we get another round?"

Before I could answer, someone bumped me from behind, and I put a hand on Hunter's chest to steady myself. Beneath his shirt, he was hard and muscular; he definitely wasn't skimping at the gym.

I swallowed, tempted to grip his shirt in my hand and pull him toward me. Instead, I stepped away, mentally composing myself. I usually didn't get tripped up this easily by a guy, but there was something about him that had my heart fluttering like a teenager. I didn't want another drink . . . I wanted Hunter. Plus, I was worried one more round with him would push me from being adorably tipsy to embarrassingly drunk.

"Maybe we could just get out of here?" I said slyly.

He seemed caught off guard for a second but quickly composed himself. "We could also do that."

Nervous and excited, I told Hunter I'd meet him out front, and went to find Jessie and Rebecca. They were huddled in a corner of the bar and had obviously been watching the whole thing.

"He looked super into you," Jessie said enthusiastically as I walked up.

"We're going to his place." I grinned. At least, I hoped we were, because I was sort of homeless at the moment. And I was fairly certain that hooking up on your soon-to-be-ex-roommate's couch was frowned upon.

"You go, girl." Rebecca gave my butt a little slap.

I pulled them into a quick group hug. "Love you guys."

"Tell us everything tomorrow," Jessie said, shooing me toward the door.

Hunter was out front waiting with a cab. He opened the door for me and I climbed in, thinking I'd never met someone this hot who also had manners.

I was way too aware of how close we were as we sat in the back of the cab, tension building with the unspoken agenda that was playing out right in front of us. Unable to stop myself, I scooted next to him, my body resting closely against his. His hard chest pressed against my shoulder, and I inhaled sharply as he put an arm around me. My body reacted instantly, my lady parts firing on all cylinders.

He ran his fingers along my shoulder and down my arm, such an innocent touch, yet it held the promise of so much more to come. My hand gently stroked his oh-so-very-muscular thigh, my gaze slipping over the rest of him as I did. If the bulge in his pants was any indication, he was very well endowed.

I swallowed, suddenly light-headed from how much I wanted him. The liquid courage I'd consumed earlier was in full effect. If he could make me feel like this fully clothed in a cab, I couldn't help but wonder what he could do in the bedroom.

It was a short ride, but by the time we pulled up to Hunter's two-story colonial, I didn't think I could wait any longer.

He pulled out his keys at his front door and paused. "I should probably warn you. I have to pay the babysitter."

"The babysitter?" My mind, a little fuzzy from all the tequila shots, wasn't catching on. Was this some weird sex fetish?

"I have a daughter," he said, seeming nervous. "Is that okay?"

Normally, I wasn't much of a kid person. But I was drunk and had been picturing Hunter naked for the past two hours, so I wasn't about to make a fuss about any offspring he might have.

"Of course. That's fine with me," I said quickly, and he let out a sigh of relief.

We stepped inside, and I peeked around while he paid the sitter. There were pictures of him with a small, dark-haired girl. I briefly wondered about her mother. I wasn't here to get his life story, though; I was here to cash in on a tradition called birthday sex.

When the babysitter glanced at me as I was looking at the photos, I did my best to seem like I belonged here, and that Hunter and I weren't about to have a super-classy, drunken one-night stand. After speaking quietly with Hunter for a couple of minutes, she finally left.

He pulled off his suit jacket, his well-defined chest and biceps straining against the fabric of his shirt. I walked toward him, more than ready to start my birthday off with a bang.

If this was how I was ringing in my thirtieth birthday, it was about to be the start of a very good year.

Chapter Two

Hunter

Maybe it was the music. Maybe it was the fact I'd barely eaten dinner, on top of drinking, when I never drank much to begin with. Or maybe I'd just been a little pent-up after a six-month dry spell spent having tea parties and braiding my four-year-old daughter's hair. Whatever the reason, there was only one thought running through my mind the first time I laid eyes on Kate from across the bar.

I want her.

And once I saw her in that skintight dress, doing a horrible job of pretending to not be checking me out? I got all kinds of ideas about how to expend that pent-up energy. And now we were here, standing in my living room, surrounded by photos of my daughter. Which was pretty much the exact opposite of an aphrodisiac.

When we'd climbed out of the cab, I'd realized that the topic of my daughter never came up in our bar banter—and that we were about to be confronted with the babysitter. There really wasn't any way around it.

Casual flings didn't tend to handle the whole single-dad thing well. Single moms, on the other hand, fucking loved it. The idea of a man devoted to his kid had them panting for days. But casual, no-strings hookups? To them, me being a dad screamed one of two things: I was either an irresponsible asshole who couldn't properly wrap it up, or I was a total commitment addict trying to lure them in with my adorable four-year-old child in need of a new mama. Either way, it usually didn't go over well. But so far, Kate was handling it fine.

Then she crossed the room toward me, and a single thought pervaded my brain.

Fuck, she's sexy.

All those curves and her throaty laugh, coupled with her confidence? I was a total sucker for a confident woman who knew what she wanted.

"Happy birthday," I whispered, placing my hands on her waist and drawing her in close.

Just because this would most likely be a one-time thing didn't mean I wanted to rush through it. Quite the opposite, actually. I wanted to savor and enjoy every minute of this. Starting with the perfect kiss.

"It's almost midnight," she murmured, her lips just inches from mine.

Placing one hand on her cheek, I guided her mouth to mine, sealing my lips over hers in a slow, soft kiss.

She responded perfectly, opening her mouth in a silent invitation for my tongue to slide against hers. My hands found those curves wrapped under that black fuck-me dress I'd been admiring, and God, she felt even better under my palms than I could have imagined. Soft and warm and so inviting.

I pressed one more slow kiss to her lips and pulled back to study her reaction. I rarely did this kind of thing. Having her here was surreal . . . and really fucking turning me on, knowing what was probably about to happen.

"Can I get you something to drink?" I asked, slipping my hand around her waist. If she'd changed her mind or wanted to slow things down, I wanted her to know that was fine too.

"I can think of other things I'd rather be doing with

"Oh fuck, are you okay?" I paused, leaning back slightly to check and make sure she wasn't injured.

She chuckled. "Yeah, I'm fine. It didn't hurt; it was just loud."

Smiling, I bent down to kiss her again.

As the kiss grew hotter, her tongue stroking mine, she began unbuttoning my shirt with surprising ease. Within moments, she was pulling the sleeves down over my arms and tossing the shirt to the floor.

"Impressive," I murmured, moving my lips to her neck, sucking and nibbling on her skin. She tasted sweet and smelled faintly of vanilla.

"Not my first rodeo." She sighed, reaching to unbuckle my belt.

I smiled. *Two can play that game.*

Hiking her dress up over her waist, I slipped her panties off with one hand, the other returning to its previous job of pleasuring the wet, silken spot between her thighs. The desire to rub and pet her until she was writhing and mewling and out of control was so powerful, my mouth," she replied, her voice low and sultry as she ran her fingertips over my chest.

God, I love a woman who knows what she wants.

Wordlessly, I placed my hand around the back of her neck, guiding her face to mine for another sweet kiss. She wrapped her arms around me and pressed her hips into me, lining up perfectly with my quickly growing erection.

As our tongues moved more urgently together, I slowly guided her down the hallway toward the stairs. Our breathing became heavy and labored, and with each step closer to my room, my cock grew harder. I was sure she could feel it pressing into her belly as we crossed the threshold into my room.

I backed Kate up against the wall, slipping my fingers under the hemline of her dress to feel the soft, warm skin of her upper thighs. She whimpered softly, and I moved my fingers to the front of her panties, my cock twitching at the feel of her heat against my hand. Pushing her panties to the side, I found her wet already and slowly slid one finger inside, causing Kate to throw her head back in pleasure, where it collided with the wall behind her with a loud thwack.

I was almost shaking with it.

God, it's been too long.

As my hand moved between her legs, she bit her lip and let out a soft moan. Pulling at my belt, her fingers fumbled briefly over the zipper of my pants before roughly pulling them down to reveal the outline of my rock-hard cock, fully outlined by my black briefs. Her breathing became more ragged, and I knew she was ready for more.

Pausing to pull her dress the rest of the way up and over her shoulders, I dropped it to the floor. Kate reached to unclasp her bra, and then it joined the rest of our clothes. Hauling her closer, I reveled in the feel of her full breasts against my chest as her fingers tugged at the waistband of my briefs.

Suddenly, my need to be inside her overwhelmed me. I guided her to the bed, pushing my underwear off in the two strides it took to join her. Descending on top of her, I resumed kissing her neck, aligning my hips with hers as she widened her legs to greet me. But before I could slide my aching, eager cock against all that wet flesh I was craving, she pressed her palms into my chest, prompting me to flip over onto my back.

Did I mention I like a woman who knows when to take charge?

I lay down, and Kate climbed on top of me.

"This okay?" she asked.

"I'm more than happy to let you ride." My hands explored, caressing her breasts.

"It is my birthday, after all," she replied with a satisfied smirk.

"Excellent point." I grabbed a condom from the table beside my bed, tore the package open with my teeth, and handed it to her. "You want to put that on me?"

"My pleasure," she whispered, sending all kinds of chills racing down my spine.

Her clever fingers made quick work of the condom. Placing one hand on her hip and the other on my swollen shaft, I guided myself into her snug pussy, the two of us moaning at the long-awaited pleasure. She felt like a fucking furnace around me. She was so hot and so sexy perched on top of me like this.

We quickly found our rhythm, my hips pumping in a steady pace while she rocked above me. It was heaven, pure heaven. She felt incredible—so tight and warm and inviting. And the sexy, throaty moans she let out were destroying my stamina.

It was the best sex I'd ever had with a one-night stand. Her moans grew higher pitched as I found that place inside her and stroked it again and again with my cock.

Her palms flattened against my abs, and her head fell back as she lost herself in the pleasure.

"That's it, sexy girl. Come on my cock," I murmured.

But then I heard something . . . and it wasn't another of her moans.

No, it was something that made me freeze, my hips stilling in mid-thrust.

The creak of a floorboard in the hallway. Bare feet on the hardwood floors.

And then a small voice asked, "What are you doing to my daddy?"

FUCK.

Standing in the open doorway was my four-year-old daughter, Maddie, in her unicorn pajamas, her eyes wide as she clung to her favorite teddy bear.

"Fuck, oh my God, fuck, I'm so sorry!" Kate quickly climbed off me, grabbing the nearest blanket to cover her naked body.

"Hey, sweetie. What are you doing up?" I said in my calmest voice, frantically covering my quickly dying erection with a pillow.

Kate was running around the room trying to find her clothes. Suddenly, the haphazard way we were throwing them around seemed incredibly stupid.

"Daddy's fine. Why don't you go wait in your room, okay?"

Maddie scowled but obeyed, throwing one last dirty look in Kate's direction before turning and walking back to her room.

Kate didn't seem to notice, however, as she'd finally found her underwear and was getting dressed faster than I thought was humanly possible. She could have literally won the world record in getting dressed.

I pushed my hands into my hair, letting out a deep sigh. Shit, why hadn't I thought to lock the door? We must have been louder than I thought if we woke Maddie. She was normally a very sound sleeper.

"Listen, Kate, I'm so—"

Before I could finish, she ran out of the room, and twenty seconds later, I heard the front door open and slam behind her.

I sighed, burying my face in my hands. *Perfect, just fucking perfect.* Another casual fling ruined by being a single dad.

I was used to a few bad dates every now and then, like getting a *your daughter just threw up* phone call from the babysitter, but this? This was unlike anything I'd ever experienced before. I'd actually been caught in the act, doing the deed, bumping uglies—although there wasn't one ugly part of Kate, and I was really pissed I didn't get to see every part from every angle.

It was official. My four-year-old was a cock-blocker.

Sighing again, I went to my closet and pulled on some sweatpants and a T-shirt before gathering the rest of my clothes and placing them in the closet. In the bathroom, I washed my hands and checked my face in the mirror, raking my fingers through my hair so it wasn't so obvious I'd just been caught in the middle of boning a stranger . . . by my child.

Real classy.

I was a dad now. I needed to be better than this. Stronger. Keep my priorities in check. And my priority was definitely my daughter.

I opened the door to Maddie's room to find her curled up in her bed, staring at me with wide, confused eyes.

"Daddy, what was that lady doing to you?" she asked, rubbing her eyes with her tiny hands.

"Daddy and that lady were just spending some adult time together, that's all. I'll tell you more about it when you're older, okay?" *And when it's not the middle of the night and you just witnessed something that will inevitably scar you for life.*

Maddie furrowed her brow but nodded, and I could

already tell it was something she'd remember to ask about in the morning. I hadn't planned to even remotely have this talk with her for at least another ten years, so I mentally reminded myself to check my parenting books to find out what's normal to tell kids her age about sex. I didn't want her to be one of those kids who still believed storks dropped babies on doorsteps when she was fifteen, but still. Four seemed a little young to know everything about the birds and the bees.

Seconds later, Maddie rolled over and closed her eyes. I placed a kiss on her forehead and, once I'd tucked her in, left her room to get myself ready for bed. After brushing my teeth and splashing some cold water on my face, I lay down to sleep, only to find my mind racing.

I couldn't believe that things had started off so damn amazing yet had ended up so horribly. It had been so long since my last casual fling, I couldn't even tell you if I'd ever imagined something like what happened tonight actually happening. Scratch that. I definitely never imagined that my daughter would walk in on me having hot sex with someone I hardly knew.

It just figured that the one time I put myself out

there, I got burned. There were reasons single dads didn't do things like that anymore. Crazy shit like this happened.

Sighing, I flipped my pillow over, trying to relax and get comfortable. But I already knew I wouldn't be sleeping well that night. I couldn't stop myself from replaying that moment over and over again in my head, the complete shock of being in absolute ecstasy one moment, and the next . . . absolute embarrassment.

And the worst part was, Kate seemed like a really cool person. Even if she wasn't the love of my life, our chemistry was hard to deny, and I wouldn't have minded making our casual hookups a regular thing.

If nothing else, there was one thought that made me feel better as I unsuccessfully tried to fall asleep.

At least I'll never have to see Kate again.

Chapter Three

Kate

"You're joking, right?" Rebecca asked, gaping at me over her latte. I'd just recounted how my birthday hookup with Hunter had turned from dreamy to disastrous.

"I wish." I groaned, massaging my temples. Not only could I not get the image of his four-year-old daughter's horrified face out of my head, but I had a massive tequila-induced hangover. "I probably scarred that little girl for life. Is this what being thirty is like? All the guys have kids now?"

Rebecca put a hand over her mouth, unable to suppress a laugh.

"Come on, it's not funny," I said, but her laughter was infectious, and I couldn't help grinning. "Okay, it's kind of funny. Or it will be once my head stops feeling like it's going to explode."

"What did you do when she saw you?" Rebecca asked, composing herself.

"Well, after my less-than-ladylike dismount, I ran out of there as fast as I could." I shuddered at the memory, sipping my coffee. "Seriously, I probably broke some kind of Guinness world record."

"At least you're getting an apartment today," she said, her tone consoling.

I nodded, glad there was an upside to this day. "Thank God. I'm so sick of apartment hunting."

Before this one, I'd gone to see five other places, and they'd all been disasters. One had no windows, and another was basically the size of my current closet. If this place didn't work out, I was going to officially be in panic mode.

I glanced at my phone. "Speaking of the apartment, we should probably head over."

Rebecca had agreed to come with me to check out the space and meet the landlord. I'd binge-watched enough episodes of *Law & Order: SVU* to know it wasn't a good idea to do things like this alone.

Twenty minutes later, we neared the address I'd read off the email from the property management company.

"This is cute." Rebecca smiled as we drove through the neighborhood, pointing out a craftsman-style home with a sprawling garden. "I love that everyone has a yard."

It was more suburban than what I was used to, but I didn't mind. Actually, that was a good thing as far as I was concerned. The apartment I'd picked out was above a garage, which was different, but I wasn't picky at this point. I'd heard a lot of young couples and new parents were moving to this area, which would make it a nice, quiet place for me to work.

As I watched the houses go by, an uneasy feeling crept over me. I felt strange, like I'd been on this street before. Everything looked oddly familiar, which didn't make any sense because I almost never came to this area.

"Do we know anyone who lives here?" I gazed out the window, having a major case of déjà vu.

Rebecca shook her head. "Not that I know of. The GPS says we're really close."

She eased into a spot at the curb. As we climbed from the car, I looked around again, bothered that I couldn't figure out when I'd been here before. We walked down the block and turned the corner, and then I saw it.

"It's not that house right there, is it?" I asked, a knot forming in the pit of my stomach.

"Yeah, it is." Rebecca glanced at the address on her GPS. "Why?"

My chest constricted, and my stomach dropped to my knees. I was having trouble breathing. Of course, this was just my luck. I wanted to turn and run, but my legs kept moving forward, my mind too stunned to do anything but follow Rebecca.

"Kate? What's wrong?" She gave me a strange look as we stopped in front of the house.

"Look, maybe we should just leave—" But before I could even finish my sentence, the front door opened.

It was Hunter.

Rebecca's mouth dropped open, and my heart stopped. I thought I might pass out.

This place, the apartment I'd put a deposit on, belonged to Hunter. The man I had incredible birthday sex with—well, sort of, right until his daughter walked in on us—was the landlord, and I was silently freaking out.

The three of us stood gaping at each other for what felt like an eternity, Rebecca looking from me to Hunter and back again. Thankfully, she regained her composure quickly.

"Hi," she said, extending a hand to Hunter. "I'm Rebecca. I'm just here to help Kate with the apartment."

Even as they shook hands, I could feel him watching me but refused to meet his eyes. How was this happening? I was *way* too hungover to deal with this. The property management company had only referred to him as the owner; I hadn't thought to ask for a name. So much for the good karma I'd thought I had.

"I'm Hunter," he told Rebecca, releasing her hand.

I took the opportunity to look him over. He was wearing jeans and a white T-shirt. His features looked even sharper in the sunlight, his jawline highlighted by his heart-melting smile. He had a sexy five o'clock shadow, and his dark hair was messy, like he'd pushed his hands through it.

But it was his eyes that got me. Deep and mocha-colored, and so incredibly expressive. If he'd been bothered by the events of the night before, he was great at hiding it. In fact, he looked like he'd just walked out of a photo shoot.

I tried not to think about how I looked in my laundry-day black leggings and bulky sweatshirt. I'd been too hungover to shower, so I probably still smelled like alcohol. Thank God I'd thought to swipe on some mascara before I left the house.

"So," he said, turning back to look at me, his mouth tilted in the slightest smile. "Did you want to see the apartment?"

Still speechless, I could only stare at him. Were we just going to pretend this wasn't a totally insane coincidence?

The worst part was that despite being absolutely mortified, I found my heart was doing a little happy dance just being around him. It couldn't forget what had happened *before* I was forced to flee his house in shame, the part where I'd been having the most mind-blowing sex of my life.

A memory flashed through my mind of his hands around my waist, pulling me against him, then his fingers gently pushing into my hair as he brought my mouth to his.

I sucked in a breath. *For God's sake.* I gave my head a little shake, forcing myself to return to the moment. I still hadn't answered Hunter's question, but luckily Rebecca had it more together than I did.

"Of course we want to see the apartment. It seems great," she said, smiling like a beauty pageant contestant. "Lead the way."

As he walked ahead of us, Rebecca gave me a look and mouthed *get it together.* I knew I was being totally awkward, but could she blame me? I was in a state of shock.

He led us over to the garage and unlocked a side door.

"This will be your private entrance," he said, heading up the stairs. "It's totally separate from the house, so you won't have to worry about us bothering you."

He smiled at me and I flashed an uncertain smile

back, still not sold. The entrance might be separate, but we'd be living only a few yards away from each other, which meant seeing each other on a daily basis.

When we got to the top of the stairs, I almost forgot how much I didn't want to be there. The apartment was beautiful. It was small but well laid out and incredibly clean. There were dark wood floors, and huge windows that drenched the space in sunlight. A fully equipped kitchen had a little nook in front of the bay window that would be a perfect spot for my desk.

"I renovated the space myself," he said, running his hand along the kitchen's granite countertop.

"Really?" Rebecca asked. "That's amazing. Do you work in construction?"

"No." He shrugged. "I'm just good with my hands, I guess."

I could have told her that. Hunter could do a lot more with those hands than install wood floors.

Even though I wanted to hate it and rush out, my brain cataloged all the unique details—the crystal knobs on the cabinets, the built-in shelves in the living room.

He'd really taken the time to make the apartment one of a kind. I walked over to the window and let out a little gasp of excitement when I saw a small pond in the backyard. It couldn't have been more perfect. I really wanted to live here. *Fuck.*

"I'll let you two look around," he said, excusing himself.

I couldn't look at him yet, so I mumbled something and nodded. How could I live here if I couldn't even look at my landlord, let alone have a conversation?

Once he was safely down the stairs, I grabbed Rebecca's arm. "Get me out of here," I begged.

"Come on, you know this is an amazing apartment," she said, pulling her arm away. "I wish I could live here. Look at that pond; it's adorable. And the kitchen is perfect for you to cook in. Have you seen this little wine cabinet he put in?" She walked over to it, motioning for me to follow.

I nodded, not budging. "I know. It's beautiful and perfect. But can we also talk about how his daughter saw my naked body bouncing on top of her very naked dad last night?"

"Okay, yes," Rebecca said seriously, nodding. "That's an issue. But memories fade. And you're never going to find another place this nice that's this affordable."

I didn't want to admit it, but she was right. If I wanted to live here, I'd need to forget everything that had happened between Hunter and me.

"Okay, I'll think about it." I sighed, then looked around again, already mentally planning how I'd arrange my furniture. "It's going to be really hard to pass up."

"Just talk to Hunter about it," Rebecca said as we headed down the stairs. "Maybe his daughter didn't even remember last night."

I raised an eyebrow at her. I seriously doubted the little girl would forget something so traumatic, especially after seeing the way she'd reacted. She probably didn't like the idea of some new woman in the picture, taking her dad away from her. And I got that, but it didn't make me feel any better about the situation. The last thing I needed was to get into some kind of turf war with a kid.

Hunter was waiting for us when we stepped back

outside.

"I'll meet you at the car," Rebecca said quickly, waving good-bye to Hunter and heading back down the sidewalk.

Once Hunter and I were alone, I finally met his gaze, my heart frantically beating out of my chest. God, he was sexy. There was something about his eyes that made it impossible to look away. I swallowed, unable to shake the weird mix of embarrassment and desire.

Jesus, Kate. I mentally slapped myself. *Keep your pants on.*

"So," I said, breaking the awkward silence.

"Last night was . . ."

"Yeah." I smiled awkwardly.

There was a beat of silence, and then we both started laughing.

"Listen, we're both adults," he said, holding up his hands. "If you like the place, it's yours. We can forget last night ever happened."

"I really love it," I admitted. "You did an amazing job on the renovations."

"Thank you. Look, I need a renter and you need an apartment. There's no reason this has to be weird," he said, smiling.

I hesitated. "Does your daughter hate me?"

He pushed his hands through his hair and laughed, but I could tell the humor in the situation was forced. I was sure there was nothing funny about him having to explain what had happened last night when he put her back to bed.

"No, she doesn't hate you. She's just not used to seeing women around."

I had a hard time believing Hunter had any trouble getting women into his bed. But in the interest of not being homeless, I decided to believe him.

"All right." I grinned, extending my hand. "Let's do it."

When he took my hand in his, my stomach flipped. A zing of electricity passed between us, almost like our bodies were remembering what we'd been doing not even twelve hours before.

I knew I wasn't only agreeing to move in because it was a perfect apartment; there was something about Hunter that made it impossible to say no to him.

I let go of his hand and followed him inside to fill out the paperwork, hoping I hadn't just made a huge mistake.

Chapter Four

Hunter

A few days after Kate confirmed that she wanted the apartment, I was sitting in the living room with Maddie, reading the paper while she worked on assembling the latest Lego set I'd bought her. As a civil engineer, I felt it was important to buy my daughter just as many building projects as I did baby dolls.

I glanced over at Maddie and couldn't help but smile at the scrunched-up, determined look on her face. She was quite the problem-solver, my little girl, and I loved to challenge her mind with different educational toys and games. And teaching her that just because some boy called her pretty didn't mean she had to share her cupcake, and lots of other important life lessons. Although the conversation the other night was one I'd have preferred wait for another twenty years.

"How's it coming, sweetie?" I asked, setting the paper down in my lap.

"Good," she chirped without looking up, jamming

one blue Lego on top of another with a flourish. Glancing from the structure in front of her to the pile of Legos to her right, she carefully picked out a red piece and continued her slow process of deciding where to put it.

I chuckled and was about to resume reading the complaints about our city's bus stops when I heard a low rumble and a loud screeching sound in front of the house. Placing the paper on our coffee table, I stood and walked over to the window to see what was going on.

A midsized moving van was parking at the curb outside our house. And sure enough, once the van was fully parked, Kate stepped out of the driver's side door, turning to make sure she'd parked far enough over.

Gotta love a woman who likes to do it herself.

My heart rate kicked up at the sight of her, causing me to quickly look away and shake my head. I wasn't normally the kind of man who got aroused just by staring at women on the street. But seeing Kate again, after the things we'd shared on her birthday . . . well, let's just say I had a hard time keeping my thoughts clean.

Raking my fingers roughly through my hair, I turned

to get Maddie's attention. "It looks like our new neighbor is here with all her things. Should we go out to meet her and help her carry some stuff?"

"Our new neighbor is a girl?" Maddie asked, her voice high and excited.

"Yes, our new neighbor is a very nice lady. I think you'll like her a lot," I said calmly.

And I pray to God you won't recognize her in broad daylight.

Maddie dropped the Legos she was holding onto the floor, gleefully running to the closet to put her shoes on.

As I walked over to the doorway and slipped into some sneakers, I started to panic over the slim chance that Maddie would recognize Kate and what her reaction would be. What were the chances that Maddie even saw Kate's face? Maddie hadn't talked about the incident in a couple of days, and part of me hoped there was a good chance that she'd put it out of her mind for good. Or at least until she was older and in therapy.

We walked out the front door to find Kate opening the back of the van, revealing stacks and stacks of cardboard boxes lined up in front of a precarious pile of furniture. At first glance, it looked like a lot of stuff for one person, but what did I know? I was sure if Maddie and I were to move anytime soon, we'd need a van at least twice the size of Kate's.

By the time Maddie and I got to the curb, Kate had already begun her attempt to lift the boxes out of the van, standing up on tiptoe to reach the highest box. Her fingers just barely brushed the bottom, and no matter how far she stretched her arms, it was clear that she just wasn't able to reach the box.

I stood there watching for a second longer than I should have, amused by her struggle and finding it endearing, when Kate happened to turn and see us standing there watching her.

Shit. Now I look like an asshole. "Hey, neighbor, need a hand?"

I walked over to help her, easily lifting the box off the stack and stepping back out of her way. A wave of annoyance washed over Kate's face, and even though I'd only known her a few days, I was pretty sure there was a lot of determination and independence to her.

"How long were you just going to stand there and watch me struggle?" she asked, placing her hands on her hips and cocking her head to the side.

I knew we'd discussed being adults and forgetting about the other night, but damn if she wasn't sexy, even when she was a little mad.

"Well, I didn't want to question your capabilities and what sort of contortions you could twist your body into to reach that box." I smirked, raising an eyebrow at her.

Kate smiled and ran her fingers through her hair, and my mind flashed back to the way she pulled her dress over her body, her breasts bouncing softly with the motion.

Jesus, Hunter, focus.

"What is *she* doing here? Did she forget her underpants?"

Maddie's voice snapped me out of my trance, bringing me right back down to reality. *Fuck.*

I gave Kate an apologetic look and turned to shake my head at Maddie. "No, sweetie, she didn't forget anything. This is Kate. She's our new neighbor. She's going to live in the apartment above the garage."

Maddie furrowed her brow, crossing her arms with a humph. "But she was hurting you, Daddy."

I could tell by the look on her face she was close to a breakdown, and I knew I had to do something—and fast. A four-year-old having a meltdown on your first day moving into a new apartment? Didn't exactly bode well for a new tenant.

"Remember, we talked about this. Daddy and Kate were having a special adult snuggle-time. It's just not for kids, that's why Kate had to leave."

Having to re-explain all that in front of Kate was embarrassing. I quickly glanced over to give her another apologetic look. Thankfully, even though she looked just as mortified as I did, she smiled weakly at me before turning to talk to Maddie.

"Your daddy's right. It's something you'll learn about when you're older," Kate said calmly, leaning down and nodding her head.

Maddie made a sour face at both of us, shaking her head with another humph. "But I wanna know now," she whined.

It was time to pull out the big guns.

"Right now isn't the time to talk about special adult snuggles. Right now, we need a big girl to help us move some of Kate's stuff into her apartment. If you can't be a big girl, then I guess you'll just have to go inside and sit by yourself," I said in my calmest voice.

Maddie's face fell, and she then quickly perked back up. "Nope, I'm a big girl. I can help!" With a determined look on her face, she marched over to the back of the van and stuck her arms out to carry something.

Crisis averted. For the moment.

The three of us spent the next half hour walking boxes from the van up to Kate's apartment, being sure to give Maddie the lightest objects that would still make her feel involved.

Kate didn't have that much stuff after all—it just looked like a lot piled into the back of the van. But once it was all sitting in the living room of the apartment I'd spent the past couple years remodeling and making just right? I liked the idea of someone filling the space with life. There were potted plants drinking of the sun in the front windows, and kitchen gadgets on the counters.

Once everything was unloaded from the van, I set Maddie up in her room with a book for her forty-five minutes of quiet time. She'd started outgrowing naps a few months ago, but I'd found that giving her some downtime, especially after an eventful day, kept her from having meltdowns in the late afternoon.

I sat on the edge of Maddie's bed and smoothed her hair over her ear. "I'll be right back, okay, Mads? I just need to go give Kate the keys to her apartment." *And do my best not to think about her naked.*

Maddie furrowed her brow. "Are you going to have another special adult snuggle-time?"

I sighed. *You can't get anything past this kid.* "No, sweetie. We won't do that again. I'm just going to talk to her. I'll be right back."

I placed a kiss on Maddie's forehead and left her room before she could ask any more questions about that damn adult snuggle-time. I had a feeling that impulsive turn of phrase was going to haunt me until she graduated from college.

Grabbing the keys to Kate's apartment from a bowl in the kitchen, I quickly checked my reflection in the hallway mirror before walking over. We might not ever get busy again, but I couldn't deny my attraction to Kate. I smoothed the messy hair I'd yet to style today and walked through the door, ready to finally talk to my new neighbor without my daughter's eagle-eyed observation.

When I arrived at Kate's entrance, the door was slightly ajar, so I knocked lightly before gently pushing it open. "Kate?" I called, stepping through the door. "I just wanted to swing by to drop off your keys and see if you need anything."

"Be there in a sec!" Her voice came from the bedroom, accompanied by the sound of boxes sliding across the hardwood floor.

Shutting the door behind me, I wandered into the living room, where Kate had already begun assembling a bookshelf and sorting boxes. Before I could take a peek at what kind of books she liked, she came walking around the corner, her face flushed, tiny beads of sweat on her forehead.

"Thanks for dropping off the keys. I would have completely forgotten about them in all the chaos of moving." She chuckled and wiped her forehead with the back of her hand.

The combination of her flushed appearance and slightly out-of-breath voice took me right back to that night at my place, her voluptuous body pressing into mine, her lips on my skin. I could feel a stirring behind my zipper, so I promptly wandered around the room, nervous that she might notice the action in my pants and take it the wrong way.

Not that I didn't want her to think I was interested. But the last thing I wanted was to seem like a creepy landlord preying on his latest tenant.

"No worries," I said lightly, walking over to the bookshelf. "It looks like you've been busy. I'm impressed." I turned and flashed her a smile while gesturing to the newly assembled bookshelf, and I could have sworn she blushed a little.

"Well, when you live alone, you have to be able to take care of yourself," she replied, raising a playfully arched brow.

She walked to the opposite end of the bookshelf, and I couldn't help feeling like we were circling each other, testing the physical boundaries of our new dynamic.

I took a step toward her. "I don't doubt that you're more than capable. But know that if you ever need anything, I'm always available."

"Careful. *Anything* is a pretty big offer." Her mouth twisted into a coy smile.

"I mean it. Anything." I held her gaze for a few seconds longer than appropriate. *God, what I wouldn't give to just push you up against that wall right now.*

Kate smiled and chuckled softly before turning away and tucking her hair behind her ear.

Maybe I'd gone too far, but I meant it. Even if our connection wasn't serious, I was already feeling a little protective of her. She was a single woman, and if she needed a man for a job, something inside me wanted to be that man.

Running my fingers over the top of the bookshelf, I let my gaze wander over the boxes scattered throughout the room. Books, kitchen supplies, knickknacks . . . *whoa.*

“Wow,” I said as I locked on a much larger box in a corner of the room. “You have a huge vinyl collection.” I walked toward it, my eyes growing larger by the second.

“You’re into vinyl?” she asked, a smile spreading across her face.

“Big time. Do you mind if I take a look?”

“Be my guest.”

When I reached the box, I bent over and began thumbing through her records, all housed in pristine sleeves. I’d already thought that Kate was cool and sexy, but this? This was taking it to a whole new level.

“Billie Holiday, Miles Davis, the Beatles . . . you’ve got all the classics,” I said, unable to hide the surprise and admiration in my voice. I couldn’t believe that Kate liked music this much . . . or that our taste in music was so similar.

She joined me in front of the box. “I started collecting them when I was sixteen. Once I got into it, I couldn’t really stop. It’s a little out of hand.” She chuckled, rolling her eyes.

"No, no, this is amazing. Like really fucking cool." I was so floored, I didn't have it in me to be articulate. "*Paul Simon*? I love this album." I turned to look at her with wide eyes, shaking my head in disbelief.

"If you want to borrow any of them, you're welcome to. Normally, I keep my obsession with records to myself, but now that you know, I guess the cat's out of the bag—or the album's out of the sleeve, in this instance, so you're more than welcome. And if you ever want to come by for a listen, I'm only a short walk away."

"Yeah, of course, that would be great. Maddie loves this stuff too." *Shit. Nothing like bringing up your kid to kill the mood.*

"Maybe a little dance party will help her warm up to me." Kate gave me a crooked smile.

"Nah, she likes you just fine. She's just . . . adjusting." *That's one way of putting it.*

"Well, I just hope she's, uh, not scarred for life," Kate said.

We both chuckled awkwardly, and I struggled to keep myself from picturing Kate naked for the tenth time today.

"She'll be fine," I said, placing the record back in the box. "That reminds me, I should probably get going. Maddie's quiet time is ending soon, and she'll be upset if I'm not back when she comes out." That, and if I stayed in Kate's apartment any longer, I wasn't fully confident I'd be able to avoid making a move on her.

"Right, of course. Thanks for stopping by," she said, walking me to the door.

As I stepped outside, I turned to wave awkwardly before turning the corner around the garage, my heart beating fast. Kate waved back, smiling softly, and shut the door.

Back at my house, I had about ten minutes left before Maddie came barreling out of her room, insisting that she didn't need quiet time anymore. I took the few minutes of silence to collect my thoughts.

I could already tell that I was in trouble when it came to this woman. No matter how badly I wanted to forget what happened between us, every time I was around her, I couldn't keep my mind from wandering to the sight of her naked body, the feel of her slick warmth around me. And that vinyl collection? It wasn't helping anything either. She was sexy and interesting. And living mere yards away from me.

I had to find a solution to all this pent-up sexual energy, and fast.

Chapter Five

Kate

The air conditioner in the apartment had decided to die on me on the hottest day of the year so far. Worse, I was struggling to pull off the tape I'd used to roll up my gray shag rug.

I'd moved in my things a few days ago, but between writing my column and several long meetings with my editor, I'd barely even been in the apartment, never mind unpacking everything. Now, after an afternoon of rearranging furniture and unpacking boxes in the heat, I was sweating like I'd just run a marathon.

I'd stayed motivated by telling myself I could have a cocktail once I got everything done, because I was definitely going to need one. I didn't do well in heat—the only place I liked to get this hot and sweaty was in the bedroom.

Despite the setback with the air conditioner, I was excited about the way the apartment was coming together. I hated to admit it, but I was starting to appreciate suburban life. It was so quiet out here, and I was getting the best sleep of my life. Maybe I was just getting old and boring, but watching the little ducks splash around in the backyard pond was my new favorite hobby.

It was a great apartment, and if I could just get it all unpacked, I'd finally be settled.

There was only one way to deal with this situation if I didn't want to melt into a puddle. I stripped off my soaking-wet T-shirt and shorts, opting to unpack in my bra and panties, and splashed some cold water on my face. I dug my portable speaker out from the bottom of a box and put on my "happy" playlist. I'd never lived in my own place before, but I had a feeling I was going to like it. Especially if it meant I could hang out in my underwear listening to Bruno Mars anytime I wanted.

I looked out the window between the shades and noticed Hunter's car in the driveway. I hadn't seen him since our last awkward encounter, when Maddie had first realized that the random woman she'd caught straddling her dad had moved in. We'd ended the night normally enough, but I still felt uncomfortable about the whole thing. He and I had almost had a run-in the other day as I was getting in my car to meet my editor, but I'd pretended not to see him. I told myself I wasn't avoiding him; I'd just been busy and hadn't had time to make small talk.

As if on cue, Hunter stepped out his front door carrying a trash bag, and I jumped away from my window, my heart racing.

Okay, so maybe I was avoiding him. But it seemed like I couldn't be around this guy without making a fool of myself, so I wasn't exactly in a rush to see him.

"Uptown Funk" came on and I grinned. This was the perfect song to make me forget all the drama with Hunter. Yes, I knew it was overplayed, but I still loved it and couldn't sit still when it came on. I might be a thirty-year-old woman, but I still knew how to get down.

I was just getting into the chorus, doing my best reenactment of the music video and holding up a wooden spoon as a microphone, when I heard a voice behind me. I spun around, mid hip-thrust, and saw Hunter standing in the doorway. We stared at each other for a moment as he took in the scene.

And that scene wasn't a flattering one. I was in a

basic white cotton bra and a pair of neon-green boy-shorts with penguins all over them.

"Oh my God," I shouted as Hunter stood gaping. I dove for my T-shirt.

"Shit. I'm sorry," he said, turning to look at the wall as I pulled my shirt on. "I didn't realize . . . The door was open." He trailed off, standing uncomfortably as I snatched up my shorts.

Seriously? This was the second time I'd had to rush to put my clothes on in front of Hunter in the past week.

"It was hot, so I opened the door. I guess I forgot about it," I said, mortified and trying to ignore my flaming cheeks. I couldn't have embarrassed myself more in front of him if I'd tried.

"Sorry," he said again, once the music was off. "I was coming by to check on the A/C unit. It tends to blow its fuse on really hot days like this."

"Yeah, I noticed." I fanned my sweaty face. I was still recovering from the shock, but I managed to put on a smile. "But thanks for coming to check on it. My last landlord would have let me die of heat exhaustion before fixing anything."

"No worries." Hunter smiled. "I know it can get pretty hot up here. Do you mind if I take a look at it?"

"Of course." I gestured toward the fuse box on the wall.

He unplugged the air conditioner, flipped a few switches, then bent down to plug the air conditioner in. It immediately hummed back to life.

I grinned as cold air breezed past me. "That was amazing."

I made eye contact with Hunter, and my stomach did a somersault.

"I usually wear clothes," I added quickly, hoping my face wasn't as red as it felt. "But it was hot, so, you know. And then that song came on."

Jesus, Kate, stop talking.

He laughed. "Don't worry about it. It's my fault for just walking in. I should have called first."

"So," I said, desperate for a subject change. "How's

Maddie?"

"She's good." He smiled, and his eyes lit up like they did every time he talked about his daughter. Even though I wasn't a kid person, I had to admit it was pretty adorable. "She's watching a movie in my bed."

I raised an eyebrow. "So she kicked you out?"

He laughed. "Pretty much. She's very persuasive."

"In that case, do you want to stay and have a beer?"

He glanced out the window.

"It's okay if you can't leave Maddie alone," I said, but he stopped me.

"No, she'll be fine for a few minutes. A beer would be great, actually."

I motioned for him to take a seat on the couch while I went to grab two beers from the fridge. If we were really going to be on good terms, I'd need to spend some time getting to know Hunter the person, not the panty-dropper I'd met at a bar. Although, with how good he looked in his casual jeans and T-shirt, that was going to be easier said than done.

I handed him a beer, and he took a long swig.

"Long day at work?" I asked.

He swallowed. "Is it obvious?"

"You look a little tense, that's all."

"So, she's beautiful and perceptive," he said, and my heart skipped a beat.

I looked down at my beer bottle, suddenly at a loss for words. Still, I could think of a few things I'd like to do with Hunter, and most of them didn't require clothing.

"So," I said, eager to get my mind onto a safe topic. "What's new in transportation?"

"Nothing exciting." He smiled and took another swig. "We've just been trying to meet this deadline, and it's not going well. But seriously, you don't want to hear about it. Even I'm bored by it."

"Okay, so, what's new in life? Any girl drama?" I paused, realizing what I was saying, then added sheepishly, "Well, other than me."

After a beat of silence, we both laughed, and relief

washed over me. It seemed like we were finally moving past the awkwardness of that situation.

"Not much else. You pretty much took the cake on that one."

Still laughing, I said, "It wasn't my finest moment."

"At least you'll never forget what you did on your thirtieth birthday." He grinned.

"Thank God I'll always have that memory to cherish."

Still grinning, he ran a hand through his dark hair. I watched him, trying not to get distracted by those expressive eyes and how perfect his full lips and straight white teeth looked when he smiled.

I'd never gotten turned on by a guy's lips before, but something about Hunter's made it impossible not to think about kissing him. I was too aware of how close we were, close enough that I could easily swing my leg over to straddle him. I struggled to keep my breathing even as I imagined his hands grabbing my hips, pulling me closer as I rocked against him. It didn't help that I knew exactly how good he felt, could still feel his hands on my skin, his mouth possessing me.

Fuck.

Luckily, Hunter interrupted my thoughts before things got too dirty.

"What about you?" he asked. "What's the latest celebrity gossip?"

"That's privileged information." I smiled coyly. It wasn't, really, but I didn't think he'd be interested in hearing about who Jennifer Aniston was dating.

"Okay, let me guess. Taylor Swift has a new boyfriend, and Justin Bieber embarrassed himself at a club."

I snorted.

"Am I close?" Grinning, he took another sip of his beer.

"I didn't peg you for the kind of guy who's up-to-date on celebrity gossip." I laughed.

"I have a daughter. She's only four, but somehow she knows everything."

I grinned. "That's impressive. Maybe I should hire her to be my assistant."

"She'd be in here telling you how to write your column on the first day."

I laughed and took another sip of beer, feeling like the heat had turned up again in the room. I couldn't deny it, though. The butterflies were definitely still there, despite my best efforts to keep things platonic.

I'd never felt like this before around a guy, especially after the way our hookup had gone. In fact, even when things went well with a guy, I usually got bored with them after a week or two. Then again, neither of us got to finish that night, so maybe I was just recovering from the lady version of blue balls. In a few weeks, the tension would ease, and hopefully I wouldn't be imagining jumping into bed with him every five minutes.

"I should probably get back and make sure Maddie hasn't set the house on fire." He stood up and stretched, and his shirt lifted just enough for me to sneak a look at his hard-as-rock abs.

I bit my lip. *No, Kate.* I mentally slapped myself. This

was exactly the kind of thing I needed to stop thinking about. Too bad I could still remember how those abs felt under my hands as I rode him.

"See you around." I smiled, trying to pretend I wasn't remembering what his cock felt like inside me, and walked him to the door.

"Thanks for the beer," he said, then added with a sly grin, "And let me know if you need anything up here. Judging by what I saw earlier, you seem to be having a pretty good time so far."

I slapped his shoulder and snorted a laugh. "You're not allowed to tell anyone about that."

"Okay, my lips are sealed." He smirked before heading down the stairs.

Once he'd left, I collapsed on the couch, trying to recover from the roller-coaster ride that was my attraction to Hunter. But it was nice to know we could have fun together without getting horizontal.

I resolved to work even harder to keep our relationship strictly landlord and tenant. After all, I was a classic commitment-phobe; I couldn't even commit to a cat or a signature lipstick color. What did I think I was doing fantasizing about getting involved with a guy who had a kid? I wasn't committed to being a stable role model for his daughter, and it wouldn't be fair to him or her to blur the lines in our relationship, especially when things inevitably went south.

As much as I wanted to tear my clothes off and finish what we'd started the week before, I'd have to keep it PG, no matter how cute and helpful Hunter was.

Chapter Six

Hunter

"No, no, no, there's no way I'm letting you wear that on a date," Kate said, crossing her arms and shaking her head.

I'd just walked out of my bedroom to show her what I'd thought was a reasonable outfit for a casual *let's start with drinks and see where this goes* kind of date. But based on the horrified look on her face? I was dead wrong.

"What's wrong with this?" I asked, gesturing at my khaki pants and blue plaid shirt. I wouldn't have gone so far as to call myself a style expert, but I didn't think this outfit was *that* bad.

Kate's eyebrows shot straight up, her eyes growing wide with disapproval. "Khakis?" she exclaimed. "For drinks?"

"They're nice," I said defensively, brushing the front of my pants with my palms.

Kate softened for a moment, uncrossing her arms

and sighing. "They *are* nice," she said, leaning forward from her spot on the couch to take another sip of her glass of wine, "if you're going to church on a Sunday and a picnic afterward. But you're going on a date. I beg of you, go try again." She nodded authoritatively, scrunching her brows together in a determined look.

"Fine," I muttered, turning to head back up the stairs. But I had to admit a part of me was getting a kick out of this, recalling the way she'd called me out on my cheesy pickup lines that night at the bar.

"Go put some jeans on. Dark wash, please!" she called after me as I rounded the corner to my bedroom. "And nothing too baggy," she called again.

Unbuttoning my shirt, I couldn't help but smile and shake my head at how comfortable Kate was bossing me around. We'd only been neighbors for a couple of weeks, but it felt like we'd known each other for years. Even if things between us had a rocky start, it was nice having another adult around to share a drink with. Just having someone to talk and laugh with made the house seem not too quiet.

The only slight hiccup was Maddie. It wasn't that she

didn't like Kate, but she was still suspicious about the whole special adult snuggle-time thing, something we had to tread lightly around.

Tonight, however, Maddie was with her grandparents, most likely getting spoiled out of her mind. When it was clear Maddie's mom wasn't going to be a part of the picture, I made sure to move the two of us closer to my parents. Honestly, having them on hand was a godsend. I loved my life with Maddie and wouldn't trade our time together for the world, but the fact is, I needed backup reinforcements sometimes, no matter how much I might like attending tea parties and wearing tiaras.

Standing in front of my open closet, I pushed some shirts around on their hangers, looking for something more suitable for drinks. After tossing a pair of dark jeans on the bed, I continued rummaging around in my closet, finally landing on a gray sweater. I quickly changed into the new outfit and returned to the living room, ready to be playfully insulted by Kate all over again.

I walked out in front of the couch to find her waiting for me with her wineglass in hand. Smiling, I raised a curious eyebrow, and she quickly set the glass down on the coffee table in front of her. Before I could say anything remotely teasing, she stood with a high-pitched squeal, clapping her hands and nodding with approval.

"Look at you! This is perfect. The jeans are great, and that sweater . . ." Kate's gaze slid over my pecs and shoulders, her expression shifting just enough for me to feel a slight jolt of electricity between us. "It's great," she said quickly, snapping her eyes up to mine and forcing a smile.

"Glad to see you approve." I smirked.

She laughed and swatted my arm with the back of her hand. Even as she settled back into her seat on the couch, seemingly casual and unfazed, I could still feel the spark between us.

"Hey, your phone buzzed while you were changing. I didn't check to see who it was, no matter how nosy I wanted to be." She raised her eyebrows, a devious smile spreading across her face.

"One more glass of wine, and you'll be hacking into my phone in a heartbeat." I picked up my phone and typed in my passcode. It was a text from Heather, the woman I was supposed to be meeting for drinks in thirty minutes, telling me a work emergency had come up and she wouldn't be able to make it on our date after all.

I sighed. "Well, I hope you don't have plans for the rest of the night. My date canceled, and there's no way I'm wasting a kid-free night."

Kate's face fell, then quickly changed to something angrier. "What the hell?" she said, rising to her feet. "She's just ghosting on you minutes before the date?"

"In fairness, I'm pretty sure ghosting is when you just stop responding to someone out of the blue. At least she had the courtesy to let me know this was over before it started." I grabbed my glass of wine from the coffee table and took a seat on the couch.

Kate's angry expression morphed to one of outrage. "Why don't you seem surprised? Or mad?" She paced around the living room while gesturing at me emphatically.

"Because I'm not," I said between sips of wine. "It wouldn't be the first time a date pre-screened me on social media and learned I was a dad." *That's why sometimes it's better to make these things a little more spur of the moment, like picking someone up at a bar.*

"That's bullshit." She scoffed, plopping herself down on the opposite couch cushion, her brow furrowed in frustration. "So, you think she canceled because you have a kid?"

"Maybe, maybe not. But it happens more often than you'd think. Wait a second. Isn't that your hangup too?" I gave her a quizzical look.

"Well, no. I'm just, I'm not looking for anything serious." She stumbled over her words, obviously flustered by my question. "With anyone," she added, more to herself than to me.

I gave her a disbelieving look. "So you're telling me that if I wanted to have a fling with you—purely sexual, no strings attached—you'd be game?" As I spoke, I leaned toward her on the couch, aware again of that spark crackling between us.

She stared at me wide-eyed for a moment before blinking. "You and I are both old enough to know that *that* would be a *terrible* idea."

I held her gaze for a moment longer, memories from that first night we met flashing through my mind. Maybe she was right. Maybe a casual fling with my new tenant was a terrible idea. And yet . . . maybe it was exactly what we both needed.

I stood and picked up our empty wineglasses. "Casual sex or not, I just got stood up for a date, and that can only mean one thing."

"What's that?" she asked, crossing one perfectly sculpted leg over the other.

"It's time to order takeout."

•••

Two more glasses of wine and one large pizza with mushrooms and olives later, Kate and I found ourselves sitting at my kitchen table, tears streaming down our faces as we laughed.

"You did not," she said, her face red, wiping a tear from the corner of her eye.

"What else was I supposed to do? Maddie had pooped her pants, we were in the middle of a forest, and in my rush to get us out the door for our nature day, I'd forgotten to pack her an extra pair of clothes." I waved my hands in surrender.

It was the old *my daughter shit her pants, so I had to tie a T-shirt around her waist like a loincloth for the rest of our hike* story. Not one I was usually able to whip out on a first date.

"You're unbelievable," Kate said through giggles, shaking her head and swirling the wine in her glass. Her cheeks were rosy from the laughter and the wine, and her hair had fallen loosely around her shoulders, slightly tousled now that she was sufficiently tipsy. I'd known she was a bombshell from the moment I saw her at the bar all those nights ago, but in this moment? She wasn't just hot. She was beautiful.

"So, tell me, Kate," I said, cocking my head to the side and squinting at her slightly, "how'd a girl like you end up living above my garage? Did you dump some poor bastard and leave him to fend for himself in the uptown loft you used to share?" It was definitely the wine making me bold, asking the questions I'd been keeping to myself for weeks.

She smiled and shook her head. "No, it wasn't anything so exciting or dramatic—for me, at least. My roommate just got engaged, and it turns out, newly engaged couples don't really want another roommate around to cock-block them all the time."

I nodded. "That makes sense, I guess. So there really isn't anyone you were leaving behind? You're just a commitment-phobe through and through?"

"Well, I wouldn't call myself a commitment-phobe, although my friends probably would," she replied with a shrug.

Leaning back in my chair, I crossed my arms and gave her a long, measured look. "Sounds lonely," I said, my tone dropping.

"That's what bars are for." She arched an eyebrow and gave me a knowing look.

"Touché."

We sat in silence for a while, watching each other with soft, curious eyes. The more I learned about this woman, the more I wanted to know, but I still couldn't tell exactly where it was all headed.

"I should probably get going," she said with a sigh, glancing over at the clock hanging on the wall behind me.

I turned to check the time, surprised to see it was nearly midnight. *Damn.* It was later than I expected.

"Well, thanks for helping me pick out my clothes, even if the date was a bust," I said as we both stood and Kate gathered her things.

"Anytime," she replied, slinging her purse strap over her shoulder. "Sorry again that bitch stood you up."

"Nah, I don't think she's a bitch. Just afraid of starting something that might get too real."

Kate looked at me, surprised. "I can't tell if that's insightful or if we're both just drunk."

We laughed as we walked to the front door, where Kate paused before opening it.

"I had a really nice time tonight," she said, looking down at her feet and tucking her hair behind her ear.

When she looked up at me, our eyes locked. That energy crackled between us again, and suddenly, I couldn't ignore it anymore.

Taking her cheek in the palm of my hand, I pulled her face to mine, our lips meeting in a deep, slow, sensual kiss. When we parted, she didn't respond for a second, the look on her face communicating that she was clearly taken aback. Keeping my hand on her cheek, I stared into her eyes, searching for a sign that she wanted this too.

Without a word, she dropped her purse to the floor and wrapped her arms around me, pressing her body into mine. I took her mouth again, deepening the kiss when she parted her lips for me. My hands landed on her hips, relishing their soft and supple shape, while her hands wandered over the back of my neck, her fingers threading through my hair.

A small moan escaped her as I moved my knee between her legs, feeling the heat straight through my jeans. My cock responded with a twitch, aching to be free, to be inside her again. To finish what we started.

I dug my fingers into her skin, wishing I could rip off the layers of denim between us. Our tongues moved faster and more urgently, and our breathing grew heavy. Every inch of my body felt electric around her, and when we kissed, it was like turning the energy all the way up.

Suddenly, she broke away, stepping back to leave a full foot of space between our bodies. For a moment, we both stood there, breathing heavily, watching each other with wide, searching eyes.

"I, uh . . . I have to go," she stammered, then picked her purse up off the floor, quickly opened the door, and marched out, closing it behind her.

I could hear her footsteps as she made her way up the stairs, the sound of the door to her apartment opening and closing. I stood in the doorway for a moment, my mind still charged with the electricity of that kiss.

Once I'd caught my breath and my mind stopped racing, I walked back into the kitchen and began the process of cleaning up. As I stood over the sink, rinsing the wineglasses, I thought about the look on Kate's face right before she ran out the door.

Was it shock? Was it the look of someone who wanted more but knew she shouldn't? I didn't know what it meant, and I didn't know where this was going, but the one thing I did know?

I wanted to do that again and finish what we started.

Chapter Seven

Kate

I quickly ran a brush through my hair and checked my teeth for lipstick stains before running out the door. I had to go into the city for a meeting with my editor this morning, which I was dreading. He'd already been on my case all week about finishing my column, and the last thing I needed was to be late. I'd been so distracted by moving and unpacking that I'd had a hard time sitting down to get work done. And if I was being honest, my attraction to Hunter wasn't helping one bit.

After our kiss, I'd been so hot and bothered that I'd tossed and turned all night. The more I thought about it, the more I wanted to throw caution to the wind and see where this attraction would take us. After last night, the idea of giving in to the temptation of Hunter was too powerful to resist. Why not take a risk? He'd said so himself; it didn't have to lead to anything serious. We were both adults who had needs. And besides, I was never one to leave unfinished business.

Distracted, I weighed my options throughout my meeting. It was hard to focus on anything but Hunter's proposition. Had he been serious? Would he really want a casual fling? But my meeting went smoothly, and I took it as a good omen.

That night, after I'd showered and changed, I decided to stop by Hunter's place to talk to him for a few minutes. It had become part of my ritual, and one I looked forward to. As I swiped on some mascara, it occurred to me that he might have only made that comment about us casually hooking up because of the wine, or because he'd just been stood up. Maybe it sounded good in theory, but when it came down to it, he might decide he wasn't interested enough to muddy the waters of our relationship.

Annoyed at how my hand holding the mascara wand trembled, I put aside the mascara and took a deep breath. *Calm down*, I told myself.

This was so not like me. I never sat around wondering what a guy thought about me. In the past when things didn't work out with someone, I always knew it was for the best. Knew that I was moving on to the next chapter of my life, and did so with no regret.

In fact, I considered it a point of pride that I'd never had my heart broken. I'd never been the kind of woman who was afraid to say what she thought, or worried what a man thought about her, and I didn't intend to start now.

With new determination, I took a deep breath and pulled on my sandals. Pausing before I walked out the door, I hoped I was doing the right thing.

Hunter opened on the first knock. I was still taken aback by how sexy he looked every time I saw him, and tonight was no exception.

"Hi," I said, smiling.

"Hey, Kate. What's up?"

I sucked in a breath as I looked into his sexy, dark eyes, and watched as a smile transformed his face. I was about to open my mouth and spill everything I'd been thinking, but then Maddie's head popped around the door.

"Oh, it's her," she said, turning to go back inside with a frown.

"Maddie," Hunter said in a warning tone, but she'd

already walked away. He turned back to me with an apologetic smile. "Sorry about that. Is everything okay?"

My smile faltered. I was such an idiot. Why did I think I could just barge in here and blurt out my feelings? Obviously, Maddie was home. I needed to get it together; I was letting my desire for Hunter cloud all rational thought.

"Hey." I grinned, changing gears. "I just wanted to come down and ask if you'd be in for an after-work drink later tonight."

"I would, but we're kind of in the middle of a dilemma over here," he said, gesturing inside.

"Is everything okay?" Horrified, I frowned. Not only had I made a mess of this whole thing, but now I'd interrupted some kind of family emergency. *Awesome.*

"No, sorry, nothing like that. I didn't mean to sound dramatic. It's more of a kitchen emergency than an actual emergency." He laughed, and my stomach did a little flip of relief.

"I'm gluten-free now." Maddie had come back, holding a cookbook. "But he doesn't know how to make anything." She pointed up at Hunter, who laughed.

"I've suggested at least five things, and you don't want any of them," he said, half amused, half exasperated. He shot me a pleading look.

"They all sounded bad." The little girl wrinkled her nose.

She was actually quite cute when she wasn't throwing daggers at me with her eyes. I could see the resemblance to her father with her dark eyes fringed in darker lashes and soft brown hair that couldn't decide if it wanted to curl or lay straight.

"I'm actually gluten-free too," I said, hoping that maybe I could be useful for once. "I could help you guys. I cook all the time."

"That would be amazing," Hunter said quickly, the relief on his face obvious. "We've been going back and forth like this for an hour."

Maddie gave him a skeptical look but didn't say anything. Hunter motioned me inside and I followed them to the kitchen, where a bag of groceries sat on the counter.

"I got a bunch of gluten-free stuff," he said, pulling a random assortment of items from the bag.

We looked it over. There was gluten-free spaghetti, a few potatoes, and a bag of quinoa. I raised an eyebrow at him. That was it?

"I have no idea what I'm doing," he admitted.

"Don't worry," I said, looking through what he'd bought. "I have a plan."

"Do what you need to do." He put his hands up. "I'll owe you big-time. Anything you want, it's yours."

I pulled things out of the cupboards and arranged them on the counter, coming up with a recipe as I went. I knew how difficult it could be to cook meals that were gluten-free, and I was impressed that Maddie was willing to try something new. Secretly, I hoped cooking for them would score me points with both Hunter and Maddie.

As I was searching their cabinet for honey, I realized they were staring at me.

"You two can go relax. I've got this," I said, turning to wave them away after grabbing chicken breasts from the refrigerator.

Maddie ran out the patio door into the backyard, where she started kicking a soccer ball around.

"Sorry, she's still a little on edge around you," Hunter said.

"It's totally fine." I waved away his concern. "She keeps me on my toes." If I was being honest, now that the mortification had worn off, I was starting to think it was kind of funny. I liked that Maddie had a little spunk.

"Is there anything I can do to help?" he offered. He was still wearing his work clothes—a dark blue suit with a white button-down shirt, which he wore very well. He'd been wearing a suit the first night I met him.

The only thing he could do to help put out this fire was to bend me over the kitchen table, but of course I couldn't say that.

"I've got it. I can get a little bossy in the kitchen, so it's probably for the best that you don't witness that."

Mostly, I just needed to get him out of here so I could focus on cooking dinner instead of thinking about spit-roasting his sausage with my tongue.

"Why does that not surprise me?" He chuckled.

I'm also bossy in the bedroom, but you already know that, I thought, but I bit my tongue. There would be plenty of time for dirty talk later. That is, if everything went the way I hoped it would.

I tried not to think about it as I cut the potatoes and fried the chicken. Luckily, I got so in the zone when I cooked that I was able to subdue my overactive libido. I was surprisingly comfortable in Hunter's kitchen, and it was nice to cook for someone else for a change. I loved trying a new recipe, but it was less exciting when there was no one to share it with. Cooking for one was just plain boring, so a lot of nights, I skipped it altogether.

An hour later, I'd prepared a full meal that I hoped would be kid-friendly enough for my little frenemy, at least. My version of chicken tenders seasoned with honey and garlic, roasted potato salad, and a flourless chocolate cake for dessert.

Hunter had insisted that I stay and eat with them, and I hadn't refused.

"This is amazing," he said after swallowing a bite of chicken. "This is gluten-free?"

"It is. I've been making it for years. And thanks." I smiled at him, our eyes meeting. My pulse jumped like I'd missed a step.

I quickly looked away, hoping Maddie hadn't noticed. I was hoping she and I could move our relationship in the right direction, and her witnessing me drooling over her dad wasn't going to help. Luckily, she was busy eyeing her plate suspiciously. I watched as she dug her fork in and took a small bite. Her eyes widened as she chewed, and she took another bite.

"How is it, Maddie?" I asked. She clearly didn't realize I'd been watching her, because she immediately stopped chewing and shrugged.

"It's pretty good," she said in a noncommittal tone.

I had to hold back a laugh. Maybe I could eventually win her over if I kept feeding her.

"So, Maddie, how's preschool?" I asked.

"Tell her about your science-fair project," Hunter

said.

Maddie's eyes lit up in a way I'd never seen before as she described how they were learning about fossilized footprints of dinosaurs.

"We made our own fossils by putting our hands in clay, and next week we're going to the museum to see real dinosaur bones," she said excitedly, and her enthusiasm was infectious.

I grinned. "That's amazing."

She continued to describe dinosaur fossils with more passion than I'd ever seen. She even knew the proper names for dinosaurs that I'd never heard of.

After we'd eaten, Maddie ran outside to continue playing. I watched her through the window for a minute and couldn't help but smile. She was practicing somersaults, and the look of sheer determination on her face was adorable. She might not trust me yet, but I patted myself on the back for starting to get through to her.

And spending time with them was more fun than I'd expected, which only made me more attracted to Hunter. I wasn't usually into the whole dad thing, but it definitely looked good on him. His daughter was well-behaved, and he was affectionate with her, yet firm. He was a real man. One with responsibilities, a home and a child, and something about him having his shit together was extremely hot to me. It was some type of single-dad aphrodisiac I'd never experienced before.

I turned from the window so I was facing Hunter, only a handful of inches separating us.

"Maddie's too stubborn to say it, but she loved the food. She never finishes her plate like that when I cook. Then again, I barely know how to make frozen chicken nuggets."

I grinned, more touched than I would have expected to hear that Maddie liked it. "Hopefully this makes up for the trauma I've put her through."

Hunter laughed. "I'd say she's forgiven you. But seriously, thanks for this. You're a lifesaver."

There was a beat of silence. It was now or never, and I just had to hope he'd be on board. If he wasn't, at least I'd know I'd been honest. I sucked in a breath.

"So, listen. Maybe I'm reading too much into this

situation, but in case I'm not . . ." I looked him in the eye, my pulse spiking. I tried to think of a tactful way to phrase it, then decided to just blurt it out. "We clearly have an attraction . . ."

God, why is my stomach suddenly in knots? It was like being a tenth-grader all over again, wondering if a boy liked me.

Pushing forward, I said, "Maybe it's a little unconventional, but I think we're both mature enough to handle something physical between us without letting it get too messy." *Plus, it's getting harder and harder not to jump on top of you every time I see you.*

My heart fluttering, I waited, unable to read his reaction. I told myself it would be fine if he wasn't interested. There were plenty of other men out there, right?

But his face remained impassive as he watched me, and I grew more and more worried.

There might be a lot of other men, but none of them were like Hunter.

Chapter Eight

Hunter

Well, fuck me. The combination of the words Kate had just spoken and the fire smoldering in her eyes made all kinds of filthy thoughts race through my mind.

After how quickly she'd run out the other night in the middle of our smoking-hot make-out session, I'd figured that the door was closed on anything physical between us. I loved having her here, loved watching her cook tonight, and I'd spent the entire evening telling myself I was fine with things being strictly platonic.

But seeing as she just told me in no uncertain terms that she wanted to start having casual sex, clearly I was wrong. And just as clearly, I was totally and wholeheartedly on fucking board with sex of any kind with this woman. Casual, committed, tantric—I didn't care. The hard-on I'd been sporting pretty much nonstop around her was ready to take the plunge, literally.

I groaned and pushed my hands roughly through my hair. "You're killing me here. You know that, right?"

"Will you tell me what you're thinking?" Kate rested her elbows across from me on the counter, leaning forward enough to give me the perfect view of her cleavage, causing a stirring behind my zipper.

"I'm thinking that the last thing I want to do right now is play dad and put my kid to bed," I replied, my voice low and gravelly.

"Glad you're on board," she murmured, her gaze wandering lazily over my body.

"Come over after nine tonight?" If I could have pressed her up against the wall right then and there, I would have, but the last thing we needed was Maddie catching us a second time.

"Why don't you come to my place, where we know there won't be any . . . unexpected visitors," she said, moving next to me at the counter so I could feel the heat of her skin next to mine.

I groaned again and rubbed the back of my neck. "I like to be in the house while Maddie's asleep. But my bedroom door has a lock, so we won't get interrupted again. I promise," I added, turning and looking deep into her eyes.

Kate sighed and shifted her stance. I could practically see the gears working in her mind. *Please don't let my daughter be the one thing that holds you back.*

"All right," she said, smiling softly. "See you at nine."

Shortly after Kate left, I called Maddie inside to begin her nighttime routine. Thankfully, having Kate over making dinner plus an extra half hour of playtime outside had sufficiently worn Maddie out, so she was as sweet and docile as ever all through bath time and brushing her teeth.

Tucking Maddie into her bed, I pushed her still damp hair off her forehead and gave her a kiss. "'Night, sweetie. Don't let the bedbugs bite."

"I won't, Daddy." She yawned, rolling over onto her side. "Night-night."

I slowly crept out of her room, nearly shutting the door behind me. She liked to sleep with the door cracked and the hallway light on.

Walking quickly to the bathroom to freshen up, I

checked the clock. Eight fifty. I still had some time to clean up the kitchen . . . and maybe brush my teeth.

After placing the dishes in the dishwasher, I wiped down the kitchen counter as fast as I could before heading back into my bathroom. I quickly brushed my teeth and checked my reflection in the mirror. As far as I could tell, I looked the same as always, but I pushed my fingers roughly through my hair a few times for good measure.

Why was I suddenly nervous?

Just as I was debating whether I should light a candle or two to set the mood, I heard a gentle knock on the door, and my dick was standing at attention already.

Let's do this.

I opened the front door to find Kate standing there with a devilish grin on her face, her hair slightly more tousled than it was the last time I saw her.

"I was half expecting you to show up in a trench coat with nothing else underneath," I murmured, ushering her inside.

As she walked past me, I caught a faint whiff of some delicious-smelling perfume, and I couldn't help but smile to myself. The thought of Kate in her apartment only a few yards away, getting herself all primped and ready for our hookup? It was pretty sexy.

"A trench coat? Man, you clearly need to get laid more." She chuckled, turning and arching her brow at me. Even in a simple outfit of leggings and a sweater, she was sexy, and I couldn't wait to put my hands all over her curves.

"That's the idea," I replied, slipping my arm around her waist and pulling her toward me. I closed the front door and wrapped a hand around her waist, letting my fingers graze and gently squeeze her perfect ass.

She inhaled sharply and stifled a small gasp. "Not one to waste time, I see." She ran her hand down my chest and abs, stopping just shy of the growing bulge in my jeans.

"I've been waiting too long for this," I growled, my need for her becoming more and more urgent by the second. I took her hand in mine and led her to my bedroom, making sure to firmly close and lock the door behind us.

Better safe than sorry.

When I turned, Kate's gaze drifted from mine down to the obvious erection in my jeans.

"That for me?" She smiled.

I cleared my throat. "I think you know it is."

"Come here, big guy. I think we should set some ground rules first." She took a seat on the edge of my bed and motioned for me to join her.

"Okay. What did you have in mind?"

"Just want to make sure we're on the same page with everything," she said as I sat down beside her.

My skin still felt electric with desire for her, but she was right. We needed to talk about what was going on.

"Well," she said, leaning her head back and looking at the ceiling, "after the other night . . . that hot and totally unexpected kiss . . . I just realized that we clearly have chemistry. And if you're on board for something casual, and I'm on board for something casual, then what's the point in denying us both something that could be mutually beneficial?"

I smiled, unable to keep my gaze from wandering to her chest. "You make it sound like we're entering into a business transaction."

"It kind of is," she said, leaning toward me. "When it's no strings attached, you've got to make sure that each person is getting exactly what they need—nothing more and nothing less."

"Sounds like you've done this before." I gave her a teasing look.

"Casual sex does happen to be my forte," she replied with a wink. "But no, I've never done this. Officially, at least. I'm more a one- or two-night girl. Three or four if he's worth the trouble." She laughed, and I made myself laugh with her. The thought of her doing this with another man made me want to put my fist through a wall.

It wasn't that I was feeling possessive or threatened because of her experience. On the contrary, it was clear then more than ever that she knew exactly what she wanted.

Me, on the other hand, while I wasn't a stranger to the occasional casual hookup, a part of me always wondered if a connection could turn into something more serious. Something lasting. Someone who would love Maddie as much as I did.

But I knew that the minute I even hinted at wanting someone to accept me as a package deal—to love me and love my daughter—Kate would be on the first bus out of town. She didn't do commitment, and if this was all I was going to get from her, then I'd take what I could get.

I cleared my throat, realizing she was waiting for me to answer. "That's fair," I said, leaning back on my hands. "So, what exactly do you need? I want to make sure you feel comfortable."

"I just think it's best that we're always honest when we communicate," she replied, her tone serious. "The minute one of us starts lying about what we want or avoids having a real conversation, that's when this whole thing breaks down and it all becomes way messier than it needs to be."

I nodded. Honesty. I could do that. "Totally agree. Anything else?"

"Hmm." She leaned her head from side to side. "Maybe no sleepovers? Cuddling through the night is a surefire way to catch feelings."

Catch feelings? She made it sound like the plague. "No sleepovers, got it. Plus, with Maddie, that's probably not a good idea anyway."

"Exactly." Kate nodded, shifting her position on the bed so she was facing me more fully. "Any ground rules you'd like to lay down?"

I smiled, finding the intent look on her face both adorable and incredibly sexy. "I think that covers it. Honesty and no sleepovers."

I tilted her chin to mine, stealing a sweet kiss, and when her lips parted, I deepened the kiss. The feel of her tongue exploring mine had me rock hard again. It was as if my body had muscle memory and knew we were about to get another shot at this.

Pulling back for a second, I met her eyes. "You'll let me know if you want to take things to a . . . kinkier place, right? You won't just tell me to choke you in the heat of the moment without the two of us talking about it first?"

She laughed. "Choking isn't really my kink, but yes, we'll talk about it before entering into any new territory between the sheets. Any kinks of yours I should be aware of?"

"Just the usual. I'm particularly fond of oral."

"Hmm, a man who likes blow jobs. I'm stunned."

I chuckled. "Receiving is nice, but I actually meant giving."

She blinked like this surprised her. "Oh."

"I've been thinking about it for weeks. What you'll taste like, the sounds you'll make. How fast I could make you come for me," I murmured, bringing my mouth to her neck.

Kate let out a soft, need-filled noise, bringing her lips closer to mine. I leaned in, and our mouths met in a soft, warm kiss.

She moaned softly, and our kisses grew faster, more urgent. I hoisted her on top of me, swinging her legs over my hips so she was straddling me while I sat up on the bed, supporting us both.

I moved my lips again to her neck, nibbling gently on her earlobe as I slipped my hands under her shirt to unhook her bra.

Once the clasp was undone, she quickly pulled her shirt and bra over her head and tossed them across the room. My hands moved to the full, supple roundness of her breasts, massaging them gently and rubbing her nipples between my thumb and forefinger. Reveling in the feel since our time had been so fleeting that night.

She moaned, arching her spine and throwing back her head. I moved my mouth from her neck, trailing my tongue along her collarbone and dipping down to her breasts. She smelled like heaven. A warm feminine scent with a trace of vanilla. Her breathing grew heavy as she began rocking her hips over mine, the friction from our clothes making my cock stiffer by the second.

"Take these off," she said, sliding off my lap and tugging at my waistband. After unbuckling my belt, she unfastened my jeans and reached into my briefs to pull out my cock.

We kissed again, faster and rougher than before, as Kate worked her hand over my length, causing low, growling groans to rise up from deep within me.

Jesus. It has definitely been a while since a woman has taken me in her hands.

"That feels incredible."

As she continued with that motion, I took my shirt off and tossed it aside. We lay back on the bed, both moaning and breathing hard, and I slipped my hand into her pants, my fingers quickly meeting the warmth and wetness between her thighs. I rubbed along the length of her.

"You're so wet," I whispered, my voice going hoarse from the incredible movement of her hand.

"You're like a rock," she whispered back. "And I forgot how pretty your cock was."

"Pretty?" The word halted the movement of my fingers.

She laughed, looking down at her hand and slowing its movements against me. "Yes. See."

As her palm worked over my stiff length, I looked down, trying to see what she saw. A flesh-colored eight inches of thick erection that her fingers couldn't even close around. But pretty? That was a hard pass.

"Alteration to our agreement. Let's not use the word *pretty* ever again in relation to any of my body parts, especially my dick," I said, pressing my lips to hers.

"Deal."

I could have gone on like that forever, the two of us taking our time, drawing out the pleasure more than we did before. But this was our first time having uninterrupted sex, and there was no way I was letting it end with a hand job.

I shifted away from her to stand and step out of my jeans. Leaning down, I slowly peeled Kate's leggings away from her body, relishing each moment as I unveiled more and more of her soft, supple skin.

"You're so fucking sexy," I murmured, taking in the sight of her before joining her on the bed. I was more than ready for the night I'd been waiting for since the first time I laid eyes on her.

Chapter Nine

Kate

I could hardly believe this was happening. After Hunter had put Maddie to bed, I'd sneaked back over, and it hadn't taken long for things to get hot and heavy. The anticipation had only made me want him more, and we'd hardly closed the door before clothes came flying off.

I let out a soft moan as Hunter's tongue traced across my nipple. Luckily, he was as good at this as I remembered from the night of my birthday. He moved to the other breast, teasing me with his tongue as his hands slid to the waistband of my panties. I arched my back, anticipating his fingers sliding against me, but instead he moved his hand to stroke my inner thigh.

I'm going to lose it if he doesn't touch me soon.

He lifted his head from my breast, looking me in the eye as he moved his hand from my thigh to the inside of my black lace panties. He moved torturously slow before gently sliding a finger along the length of my wetness. I let out a gasp as he stroked me more firmly, tension building inside me. Hunter watched me, his deep, sexy gaze boring into mine, and as he slipped two fingers deep inside me, I let out a cry of pleasure. His fingers were touching me in all the right places, and I knew I wasn't going to last long.

And then his mouth moved lower, leaving wet, sucking kisses against my needy core until he found my clit and gave it a firm suck.

My hips almost shot off the bed at how good that felt. There was no awkward fumbling, no tentative touches. He knew exactly what he was doing, and holy hell, the man had a talented tongue.

Within minutes, I was grinding against him, whimpering softly as his tongue traced the most delicious pattern over my hot flesh.

I moaned his name and every muscle in my body tightened, my hips rocking with the movement of his fingers inside me. Just before I was about to lose all control, he pulled his hand away. I let out a whimper, aching for more.

"Need to be inside you when you come," he

murmured, placing a kiss against my inner thigh.

He moved down the bed as I tried to catch my breath, sliding my panties off before tossing them to the floor.

He rose to his knees, revealing the most absolutely perfect cock. Unable to stop myself, I sat up and reached for him, slowly stroking his length. He groaned in pleasure, and I pushed him back on the bed so I could straddle him. I moved down his body, kissing his chest, flicking my tongue across his nipples. I ran my tongue down his abs, then paused before moving it over the tip of him.

He inhaled sharply as I took him in my mouth, working my tongue over the sensitive tip. I moved my mouth slowly, taking more and more of him each time. Looking up at him, I met his eyes as I took him fully in my mouth until his cock reached the back of my throat. His whole body tensed, and I could tell he was close.

"You're killing me," he said on a groan.

I looked up and found him propped on his elbows, watching me with a worshipful expression. I loved doing this for him, making him feel good in this way. The more I'd gotten to know him, the more I knew he didn't get many shots at pleasure like this.

Hunter repositioned us so I was underneath him, then pushed my thighs apart and grabbed a condom.

The last time, he'd lain there leisurely while I rolled it onto him, but tonight was different. He made quick work of the condom and then guided himself to my center. Pressing forward, he pushed inside me. We let out a collective groan, my body shuddering with the welcome invasion.

"You feel so good." He groaned again, sliding in deeper. We were both nearly there, and it wouldn't take much of a push to send us careening over the edge we were so precariously standing on. "So warm."

I arched my back so I could take him in farther, wanting to feel him fully inside me. He moved slowly, carefully at first, and it was driving me wild with desire. He pulled himself fully out for a moment and I reached for him, needing him back, needing that connection to remain unbroken. He took my arms and pinned them above my head before plunging himself into me with an almost breath-stealing momentum.

"Hunter!"

I cried out as he thrust faster and faster, rocking my hips against him, pleasure building again in my body. I was moaning loudly, lost in the moment, and he reached up to cover my mouth with his hand, which only turned me on more. I watched him move above me as heat raced through me. We were both racing toward the finish line, and I couldn't do a thing to stop it. Wrapping my legs around his waist so our bodies were intertwined as close as they could be, I finally let go, not holding anything back as my body squeezed his and we both came.

Neither of us moved as we tried to catch our breath, Hunter's chest rising and falling against mine. After a minute, he turned his head toward me and kissed me before moving to lie next to me.

Leaning back in the bed, he said, "That was—"

"Worth the wait?" I asked, grinning.

"Definitely worth the wait. I don't remember you being so vocal last time."

I slapped him playfully. "You didn't seem to mind."

He grinned, slipping his arm around my shoulders.

I curled into him, laying my arm across his chest. I'd been worried about the after-sex awkwardness, but this was so comfortable that I was tempted to lie back and fall asleep.

This was so not me; usually after I finished having sex with a guy, I was out the door as fast as possible. Cuddling wasn't really my thing either, but with Hunter it all seemed so natural. I closed my eyes, running my hands along his firm, muscled chest. I knew I needed to go back to my own place, so I forced myself to sit up.

"I should probably get out of here," I said, slipping out of bed and searching for my clothes.

He nodded, and I thought I saw disappointment flash across his face.

"But this was great," I added as I pulled on my shirt. "At least this time, I don't have to run out in shame."

"That is a major improvement." He grinned, pulling on a T-shirt and his boxer briefs.

We tiptoed down the stairs to his front door, careful not to wake Maddie with our footsteps. I practically held my breath until I was outside—I could safely say that I never wanted her to see me in a compromising position with her dad again.

"Good night, Kate," he said, leaning against the door frame.

He looked so good standing there that I couldn't help myself; I grabbed his shirt and pulled him in for one final kiss. Even after everything that had just happened, I still felt my skin prickling and my stomach flipped. His tongue slipped into my mouth, and I gripped his T-shirt harder.

When he finally pulled back, I had to catch my breath. *Jesus, Kate, you just had sex.* I needed to get away from him before I started pulling my clothes off again.

"Good night," I said, taking a step back.

"See you tomorrow?"

I nodded, smiling, as he gently shut the door.

I practically floated up to my apartment. Letting out a

contented sigh, I lay back in my bed, mentally patting myself on the back for making the right decision.

Why had we ever hesitated to do that? Most guys I slept with didn't even know where the clit was, and the ones who did didn't know what to do with it when they found it. But Hunter . . . he was something else. And some of the things he could do with his tongue should be illegal.

I was still savoring the memory when my phone buzzed.

I think we may have broken the bed.

I let out a snort. Apparently, Hunter was still thinking about it as well.

That was nothing. I think you're going to need a new bed by the end of this.

I grinned to myself as I hit SEND.

Totally worth it.

I smiled as I drifted off to sleep. Hunter was sexy, amazing in bed, and fun to hang out with. I couldn't believe I'd thought this was going to be so complicated. Now, not only did I have a great apartment and landlord, I was living just steps away from the best sex I'd ever had.

Chapter Ten

Hunter

Kate sucked in a sharp inhale as she walked into my kitchen, staring wide-eyed at the cut on my hand. "Hunter, oh my God, what happened?"

"It's fine; it's fine. I was just trying to make cookies," I said, grabbing a fistful of paper towels to soak up the blood. Applying pressure to the cut, I raised my hand in the air above my heart. "See? All better."

"But there's no step in a cookie recipe that requires a knife," she exclaimed, dropping her purse on the counter and looking around to figure out what went wrong. "Were you trying to cut open an eggshell?"

To be fair, my hand was bleeding profusely, but it felt a little like she was overreacting. Still, watching her freak out over my well-being was kind of sexy.

"Listen, when I asked for your help with Maddie's preschool bake sale, I wasn't looking for any of your judgment," I said, raising my eyebrows at her. "Clearly, the cookies are a bust."

"When I agreed to help you, I didn't realize you were so helpless," she said, placing her hands on her hips as she surveyed the ingredients lined up on the counter. She began sorting through them all, separating the dry ingredients from the wet, before clapping her hands and looking at me triumphantly.

"I figured it out!" she said, beaming at me as she tied an apron around her waist.

"Did you bring your own apron?" I chuckled. *This woman is something else.*

"I'm choosing to ignore your mockery. I've decided to make a pie instead," she replied, cutting butter into a bowl.

"What are you doing here?" Maddie asked Kate, walking into the kitchen from the backyard, where she'd been playing outside.

"Maddie, be nice to our neighbor. Kate's here to help," I said, raising an eyebrow at my daughter as I gathered first-aid supplies for myself.

"No, it's fine. That's a fair question." Kate smiled, brushing her hair out of her face with the back of her hand. "Well, Maddie, I'm here to help with your bake sale. Your dad was trying to make cookies, but he couldn't quite figure it out. So now I'm making a pie."

Maddie nodded, looking over at me before turning and watching Kate measure out a cup of flour and pour it over the cold butter. "Does pie have gluten in it?" Maddie asked, scrunching up her nose.

"Not this one," Kate replied, turning the label on the sack of flour so Maddie could see it. "I'm using gluten-free flour for the crust, so it won't upset your tummy. Or mine," she said with a wink.

Maddie smiled and climbed up onto one of the bar stools at the counter to watch Kate more closely. Kate worked the flour and butter together, making sure to stand a little to the side so that Maddie could see what she was doing. Kate cracked an egg over the crumbly dough, mixing it together even more before turning to give Maddie a long, measured look.

"Hey, Maddie, do you think you could help me?" she asked.

Maddie's eyes widened as she nodded.

"Make sure you wash your hands first," I said as Maddie clambered down from the stool. She quickly made a beeline to the guest bathroom.

"Is that okay?" Kate turned to me. "I guess I should have checked with you first before asking Maddie. She just looked so interested. Plus, I figured it'd be good to have her finally forget about that whole adult-time thing once and for all. Give her a new memory to replace that one."

We both laughed.

"It's more than okay," I said. "I'm just hoping she didn't inherit my baking skills—or lack thereof."

I couldn't believe how easily Maddie seemed to be warming up to Kate. Once Maddie came scampering back into the kitchen, Kate rolled out the pie crust, and the two of them laid it in the tin together. For as anti-kid as Kate had told me she was, there was no denying that when it came to letting my daughter help her make a pie, she was a natural.

For a moment, I just watched them—under the

pretense of cleaning up the mess I'd made on the counter. But really, it was just such a rare thing to have a woman cooking in my kitchen, listening to my daughter's giggles as they worked together, that I wanted to linger. I hadn't dated anyone seriously enough to warrant domesticity like this since Maddie was born.

Kate and Maddie made the filling together, Kate slicing apples into a bowl while Maddie poured sugar and lemon juice over them. I did my best not to hover, but I was honestly fascinated by how easily they connected. It always bothered me that Maddie didn't have very many female figures in her life besides her grandmother and her teachers, and she was clearly enjoying herself.

The two of them continued to assemble the pie, cooking the apple slices over the stove, adding more ingredients I didn't understand to the concoction, and pouring the filling into the tin. I was shocked by how focused Maddie was the whole time, and how well she listened to Kate. It seemed to me that we might have found a new hobby for Maddie to explore when she was older.

Once they put the pie in the oven, Maddie turned

and looked at me triumphantly.

"Did you see that, Daddy? Me and Kate made a pie!" She was grinning from ear to ear, flour stuck to her face and dusted all over her clothes.

"I did see that. Great job, sweetheart." Reaching out, I gave her a high five.

"I can't wait to taste it," Maddie said, practically bouncing with excitement.

"In the meantime," I said as I brushed flour out of her hair, "why don't we get you cleaned up in time for the bake sale?"

"Can Kate come with us?" Maddie asked, looking up at me with wide, pleading eyes.

"Well . . ." I looked at Kate and back down at Maddie. "That's up to Kate. It's a Saturday, and she probably has other plans."

"Pleeease come with us, Kate," Maddie pleaded, throwing her head back and sticking out her lower lip. "I want to tell everyone that I helped you make it. No one will believe that he did it," she added, jerking her thumb in my direction.

Ah, yes, nothing like a burn from your daughter to really turn on your casual hookup.

I furrowed my brow and looked over at Kate. "You really don't have to. You've already helped us so much."

"I'd love to come. No way I'm letting you take all the credit for our awesome pie." She winked.

Maddie let out an excited yell, bouncing around the kitchen as she talked about all the people Kate would meet at the bake sale. Kate and I couldn't help laughing, watching Maddie freak out, and I walked over to stand next to Kate.

"I don't want you to feel obligated," I said to her, my voice low. "I'm going to give the little one a quick bath, and it'll be easy to make up an excuse for you. Preschool bake sales weren't really an item in our recent negotiations."

She grinned, arching a sculpted eyebrow in my direction. "I'm not doing this because I feel obligated as your buddy to pound town," she whispered, watching Maddie to make sure she couldn't hear. "I'm doing this because your daughter asked me to, and we're just starting to warm up to each other. Besides, I was serious when I said there's no way I'm letting you take the credit."

I smiled and shrugged. "Whatever you say. Just don't come crying to me when you're dying of boredom at a preschool event."

•••

An hour later, Kate knocked on our front door again, looking freshly put together in jeans and a flowy red tank top and sandals. She looked good enough to eat.

When she left to change and finish up a short article before the bake sale, she had given me strict instructions on when to check the color of the pie and how to know when it was done. Between giving Maddie a quick bath and getting her into clean clothes, I followed Kate's instructions as best I could. My one small failure was letting one side of the pie get a little darker than the other—a fact that Maddie wouldn't let me forget, no matter how many times Kate told her it was okay.

"But, Daddy, Kate and I made a pie and you messed it up!" Maddie protested, getting that look on her face that told me she was about two minutes away from a meltdown.

And I thought today was going so well.

"You're right; you and Kate did a *great* job with the pie. But like Kate said, the pie will taste fine, even if one side is browner than the other," I said calmly, smoothing Maddie's hair back, but she scrunched up her face and turned away from me, crossing her arms with a humph.

I looked to Kate apologetically. Suddenly, bringing her with us to the bake sale didn't seem like such a good idea. I was about to open my mouth to warn Maddie that our neighbor wouldn't come with us if she didn't change her attitude, when Kate walked over to Maddie, squatting down low so they were at eye level.

"I think that this pie will be even better now that your dad helped us. You and I did great putting the pie together, and your dad was a *huge* help taking it out of the oven," she said, her expression serious, then leaned in a little closer to Maddie. "And you wanna know a secret?"

Maddie nodded and leaned in.

"I like the crust a little brown on one side," Kate

whispered.

Maddie's eyes grew wide, and she stared at Kate for a moment before turning to look at me. "I guess you did good, Daddy," Maddie said shyly, looking down at the floor.

Well, I'll be damned.

"Thank you, that's very nice of you to say." I gave Kate a grateful look. "Now, who's ready for a bake sale?"

The three of us piled into my car, Kate holding the pie in the front seat while I clipped Maddie into her car seat in the back. The whole ride to the school, Maddie chattered about her friends at preschool, what their moms were making, and what treats she was hoping to buy. Kate listened politely, oohing and aahing at all the right times, while looking over at me periodically with a knowing smile.

I did my best to listen and respond to Maddie during the drive, but I couldn't help having second thoughts about bringing Kate with us to the bake sale. A lot of the moms at the preschool were . . . overinvolved, both in their kids' lives and in the lives of other parents. I was one of two single dads at this preschool, and let's just say that between the two of us, I was the one more highly sought after. I didn't want any claws coming out because the single moms thought I had a new girlfriend.

By the time we arrived at the school, the front lawn was already jam-packed with parents and their kids milling around a long wooden table, where rows and rows of baked goods were on display. Maddie quickly spotted her friends and dragged Kate and me over to them, where I introduced Kate to the other parents as our new neighbor.

"Kate was kind enough to bake this pie for us—with Maddie's help, of course," I said. "I'm hopeless when it comes to baking."

"When I walked in, he was trying to crack an egg open with a knife."

Kate snorted, already charming the hell out of the other parents. They all laughed and began teasing me about my horrible baking skills, sparing no details when it came to all the times I'd tried to pass off store-bought cookies as my own.

"You would've gotten away with it if you'd just

remembered to remove the price tag," my friend Sandra said, laughing.

Sandra was Ashley's mom, and Ashley was Maddie's best friend. The two of them were already giggling and pointing at all the different cakes and cookies lined up on the table, chattering away like only four-year-old girls can.

Just as I was about to come up with a response, someone tapped me on the shoulder. I turned to find a petite woman standing there in tight jeans and one of the T-shirts the preschool had made for the parents on the board. She was smiling widely at me and tossed her hair over one shoulder before speaking.

"Hunter, I didn't know you'd be here! Did you bake something?" she said loudly, her voice cheery and excited.

"Hey, June, how are you? No, this time around I had to call in reinforcements." I stepped back to make room for Kate in the conversation.

June gave Kate a quick once-over before smiling broadly and sticking out her hand. "Well, hi there, stranger! I'm June, Erika's mom. How do you know our Hunter?" she asked, looking quickly from Kate's face to mine, and then back to Kate's.

Our Hunter?

"I'm his neighbor," Kate said, smiling and shaking June's hand. "I didn't realize he had such a reputation for being a horrible baker."

June kept smiling, but something in her eyes changed. I couldn't help but feel uncomfortable about the way she was looking at Kate. June had been hinting that she was into me for a while, and judging by the eye daggers she was silently throwing in Kate's direction, I was guessing those feelings hadn't changed, despite the fact I'd never shown any interest in her.

"Well, Hunter," June said, her voice taking on a more serious tone, "you know you can call me anytime with whatever you need. I'm always here to offer you my *services*," she added, raising her eyebrows slightly. As she spoke, she put her hand on my arm, squeezing it slightly.

"Thanks, June, I appreciate that." I smiled politely.

June nodded and gave my arm another squeeze before sauntering away to monitor some rogue preschoolers stealing licks of frosting off cupcakes around the corner.

"I didn't realize how popular you were here," Kate said, watching Maddie and Ashley survey brownies a few feet away from us.

"Yeah, the whole single-dad thing kind of makes me stand out," I replied as the two of us wandered in Maddie's direction.

"It seems like you're a pretty hot commodity around here," Kate said.

"I guess. I think the moms are just happy to see some dads around every once in a while."

We walked in silence for a while, watching Maddie and occasionally chatting with the other parents. Kate continued to be her charming, outgoing self, but in between conversations, I could tell that something was bothering her. Suddenly, I felt bad for bringing her. I was sure that hanging out at a preschool bake sale was the last thing she wanted to do on her Saturday afternoon.

Great, drive your hookup away with how boring your life really is. Nice one, Hunter.

Maddie picked out the baked goods she wanted, and we stepped in line to pay. Kate stood with me in line while Maddie ran around the lawn with Ashley and a few of her other friends. I was happy to let her get the last of her energy out before going home for the afternoon.

"Hey," Kate said, crossing her arms and lowering her voice. "Just because we're messing around doesn't mean you can't date. Clearly, June's into you, and I'm sure a lot of the other moms here are too. If that's what you want, you should totally go for it. I'll just . . . fade into the background, no hard feelings."

Her words hit me like a sucker punch straight to the crotch. *Didn't see that coming.*

"Kate, I—"

Before I could finish, Maddie came barreling into me, wrapping her arms around my legs and laughing.

"Safe, I'm safe!" she cried, laughing hysterically as her friends formed a circle around us, clearly annoyed that they couldn't tag Maddie in their game. I gave Kate an apologetic look before looking down at Maddie.

"This is your five-minute warning, okay? It's almost

time to go."

"Aw, okay," Maddie said, still gripping my legs and leaning into me, opting to stay at my side rather than run off and enjoy the last five minutes with her best friend.

Soon, we were at the front of the line. We paid for our two brownies and slice of cake, happy to find that every slice of our apple pie had been sold.

"Told you a little brown on top makes it better," Kate bent down and said to Maddie. The two of them smiled at each other, and Maddie ran to her side to give her a small hug.

Once back at my place, I put Maddie down for some quiet time. When I came back into the kitchen, I found Kate standing over the sink, cleaning up from the pie baking earlier.

"You don't have to do that," I said, joining her by the sink.

"I made the mess. It only makes sense that I clean it up," she replied, scrubbing the last bits of crusty dough out of the mixing bowl.

I gently took the bowl and sponge out of her hands. "I don't think that's how it works."

Kate let me take them and moved out of the way, turning to stand next to me as she leaned against the counter.

"I really appreciate all your help today," I said, loading the measuring cups into the dishwasher. "I can't imagine what we would've done without you."

"Yeah, of course. Don't worry about it. It was fun," she said, shrugging with a smile.

"Also, as far as what you were saying earlier about June . . . she's been into me for a while, and she's been less than subtle about it. If I wanted to date her, I would've done that already. I'm not interested."

Kate nodded but didn't look at me, staring into the living room behind me. "Well, even if it's not her, just know that I'm okay with that. You dating someone else."

She was trying to be nice. *But why does that thought make me want to hit something?*

I took a deep breath, trying to keep any agitation out

of my voice. "I'll keep that in mind."

Chapter Eleven

Kate

I glanced out the window, looking for signs of Hunter. It was a sunny day, and I was hoping he'd be outside playing with Maddie or working on the yard. I hadn't seen him since the bake sale, and I couldn't seem to get him off my mind.

I'd tried meditation and yoga, but after my first downward dog, I gave up. I'd even considered going on a run before deciding I didn't need him off my mind *that* bad.

Something was gnawing at me, making me uneasy, but I couldn't quite put my finger on why. I thought maybe if I could just see him, I would finally be able to concentrate and figure out what was up with me.

When I tried to distract myself with work, my mind kept drifting, so I decided to clean the kitchen. Usually, cleaning and organizing relaxed me, but as I wiped down the countertops, I only grew more and more anxious. I mean, we'd had a great time at the bake sale, but suddenly

I was feeling like a crazy person.

I loaded the dishes into the dishwasher and picked up the bottle of detergent, realizing that I'd been staring blankly at nothing, completely zoned out for several minutes. After closing the dishwasher, I pressed START and walked away, determined to get out of my head.

A few minutes later, I jolted . . . there were bubbles everywhere.

Fuck. I'm losing it. I took a deep breath, worried that I was no longer adorably neurotic but had become full-blown psychotic. Whatever the case, I had a kitchen full of bubbles that needed to be dealt with.

Yeah, so I'd wanted to get Hunter's attention, but this wasn't the way I'd intended.

There was only one thing to do—I called Hunter. He came over in a couple of minutes, looking painfully sexy in jeans and a white T-shirt that fit snugly on his muscular arms.

"Shit," he said when he walked in, setting down his toolbox. The kitchen floor was filled with bubbles and soapy water.

"I'm so sorry. I have no idea what happened." I hovered behind him as he examined the dishwasher.

He stopped it and pulled it open, checking something inside. "It's fine, just too much detergent," he said, standing back up. "How much did you put in there?"

I shrugged, not wanting to admit that I'd been so distracted by thoughts of him earlier that I may or may not have spaced and dumped half a bottle of detergent inside. "I'm so sorry for bothering you. I was just worried I'd broken it or something." I smiled apologetically, hoping he didn't think I was a total idiot who didn't even know how to use a dishwasher.

"No problem. I wasn't doing much." He ran a hand through his hair, his bicep flexing.

My breath caught, and I forced myself to look away.

"I guess I'll just clean up." I grabbed a mop and some towels. "Thanks again for your help."

"I can stick around and help out."

"Are you sure? I don't want to hijack your whole afternoon."

"You didn't hijack anything. Maddie's having a play date and won't be home for another half hour."

I set aside the mop and tossed one of the towels to Hunter. Scrubbing my kitchen floor on our hands and knees wasn't the physical activity I'd envisioned in my Hunter-inspired fantasies.

Soon, we had the mess cleaned up, and Hunter sat back on his heels to survey our work. He wiped the sweat from his forehead, his shirt lifting slightly to reveal his toned stomach. He looked like he'd walked right out of a body spray commercial.

"What?" He smirked.

Damn. I'd definitely been busted checking him out.

Before I had time to process what was happening, I was crawling across the floor to kneel in front of him. Without a word, Hunter lifted my chin and pressed his mouth to mine in a searing-hot kiss. When I parted my lips in gentle invitation, his tongue slid against mine.

God, this man. He was perfection.

Large hands gripped my hips, hauling me in closer as

his tongue gently caressed mine. Then he pulled me down on top of him as he lay back on the floor.

As we kissed, I slid my hand down his body, palming his erection over his jeans. He groaned as I slipped my hand inside, wrapping it around him and slowly stroking until I could feel him throbbing in my hands. He was so thick that I couldn't fully wrap my fingers around him, and he let out low grunts as I stroked him, gripping even more tightly before finally running my finger over his sensitive tip.

"Fuck." He grunted, lifting his hips toward my touch.

"I want you," I murmured.

"Get naked." His voice was a rough growl, and it sent a thrill racing through me.

While Hunter yanked off his shirt and then pushed his jeans and boxers down, I stripped out of mine. Then he pulled my T-shirt off over my head and reached for the clasp of my bra, freeing my breasts.

He kissed me again as he cupped my breasts in his hands, slowly caressing me. He pinched a nipple in his fingers and I closed my eyes, feeling the sensation move through my body and down between my legs, where I knew I was already wet. He moved to the other breast, and I let out a low moan.

I reached out to stroke him again, the feel of how long and thick he was driving me wild with desire. I moved to straddle him, wrapping my legs around his waist, then slid myself forward until his erection pressed against my center.

I rocked my hips against him, feeling him press into me the slightest bit. He pulled me even closer, his hand gripping my hair in a knot at the back of my head as he continued to kiss me.

Unable to resist any longer, I pulled back and whispered, "I need you inside me."

He lifted me again, one hand on my hip and one gripping my ass, and then he lowered us onto the floor.

I cried out in pleasure as he pressed himself against my wetness, rubbing just the tip of his erection against me. I moaned his name softly, thrusting my hips forward, needing more. He continued to tease me, pressing just the tip of himself against me as I writhed beneath him. I ran my hands up his shoulders, all the while trying to press myself closer into his lap.

"Condom?" he asked.

Under normal circumstances, I would have felt self-conscious sprinting butt-naked to my bedroom in front of a man, but nothing about this situation was normal. I wanted him. Right here. Right now.

Seconds later, I was back with the condom.

Hunter readied himself and then pulled me close again. He stared into my eyes for a moment before rocking into me, working himself inside, moving deeper with each thrust. I inhaled sharply as he buried himself in me, digging my nails into his shoulders.

"You feel so good," he said, his voice low and husky as he stilled, enjoying the sensation of being buried inside me.

He gripped my ass, pushing himself even deeper. I gasped, every part of my body clenching. Closing my eyes, I cried out, my hips rocking against his.

We were so frenzied. I wasn't sure if it was because

his daughter was due home any minute, or because we were just so desperate for each other.

"Hunter." I groaned, inhaling sharply as pleasure poured through every inch of me.

Minutes later, a powerful release rocked through me, stealing my breath and making me contract almost violently around him.

"Shit, shit. Fuck," he cursed, still pumping into me. "Gonna come."

"Yes," I cried out, pulling his hips to mine.

His breathing changed, and he buried his face against my neck as he came.

We breathed heavily for a few minutes, our bodies slippery with sweat. Hunter reached down and brushed the hair back from my forehead as I rolled closer to him.

"Well, that was unexpected." He smiled at me and pressed a soft kiss to my lips.

"Yeah, I didn't see that coming." I chuckled.

Once he helped me up from the floor, we gathered

our clothes, and Hunter threw the condom away and washed his hands at the sink.

I stilled at the sound of a car idling in the driveway, and then a door opening.

"Shit. I think Maddie's home." He smiled apologetically as he peeked out the window.

"No need to apologize," I said, quickly dressing. "Thanks for fixing the dishwasher . . . and the rest of my plumbing." I smirked at him as he tugged his clothes on.

"Anytime." He laughed. "Just call me if you need help with that, or anything else, again."

Hunter headed toward the door, then turned back. "Also, I wanted to say thanks again for everything at the bake sale. It meant a lot to Maddie."

I smiled, touched to hear that she'd had a good time. "Of course. It was fun for me too."

He looked into my eyes for a moment, and my heart skipped a beat. How did he do that? It was like every time he looked at me, I forgot about everything but him.

After one last warm smile, he turned and walked

down the stairs.

Once I'd shut the door, I leaned back against it and slid down so I was sitting on the floor. I put my head in my hands. What was this? Was this how other people acted? Ruining their dishwasher to get a guy's attention?

I couldn't deny it anymore. I knew why I was losing my mind.

I don't want Hunter dating other people.

There it was, the cold, hard, ugly truth. I was pissed that I'd told him I was okay with him going out with that woman from Maddie's school.

I'd liked baking with them . . . *really* liked it. It felt good to be around him, and not just because he knew what he was doing in the bedroom. I even liked hanging out with Maddie, now that we were on good terms.

I stood up and looked out the window, not sure how to handle my realization.

Shit. I was in deep. I'd never felt this way before, so crazy and desperate over a guy I was sleeping with.

Was this what other women felt like when they liked

a guy?

I didn't know what exactly was happening between Hunter and me, but I definitely hadn't been expecting this twist.

Chapter Twelve

Hunter

"Here comes the *S.S. Maddie*, returning from its journey across the ocean." I chuckled, guiding Maddie's plastic bath toy from one end of the tub to the other, making chugging sounds as the little blue boat floated along.

"Yay!" Maddie squealed, splashing her arms in and out of the water in excitement.

Morning baths weren't part of our normal routine, but we had stayed up late playing bingo the night before, and I'd completely forgotten about bath time. It wasn't until she crawled into my bed for some early morning cuddles that I realized we'd forgotten it. One whiff of the top of her head, and I knew it was time to take the *S.S. Maddie* out for another voyage.

"Where did the boat go this time, Daddy?" she asked, looking up at me with bright, excited eyes.

Leaving the toy bobbing in front of her, I squirted

shampoo into my hand and worked it into her hair. As the shampoo foamed up under my fingers, I gently scrubbed her scalp, smiling at the bubbles that formed all over her head.

"Well, I heard that it traveled all the way to Iceland since the last time we saw her."

"Iceland?"

"Mm-hmm."

"Is Iceland really cold, Daddy?"

"It is, but not as cold as Greenland. Can you believe that?"

Her eyes grew wide as she looked at the little blue boat and shook her head. She then picked up the toy and started talking to it, asking how long it took to get to Iceland and if it saw any ice castles when it got there.

I rinsed the shampoo out of her hair, smiling as she splashed and played in the water. It was one of those moments when I knew I should have been watching the clock, making sure that she would get to preschool on time and that I wouldn't be late to work, but I couldn't bring myself to rush through this, or ignore how incredibly precious moments like this were.

If someone had told me five years ago that my life would be completely changed by a tiny, helpless baby coming into my life, I would have told them they were nuts. But from the moment Maddie's mom told me she was pregnant, I knew my life would never be the same.

One look at the ultrasound photo, and I was smitten. And when it was clear I'd have to raise Maddie alone, I chose to do it in a heartbeat. There was no other option for me.

My little girl became my whole world the moment I learned of her existence. Even if my personal life had taken a bit of a hit because I was busy raising my daughter, every second I spent with her was more than worth it. Maddie was everything to me, and nothing could ever take away from what we had.

The pregnancy had obviously been a surprise for us both, but Maddie's mom had no interest. Now she lived across the country and called once a year on Maddie's birthday.

Once I finished rinsing the last of the soap off her body, I helped Maddie out to dry off and pulled the plug to drain the tub. I got her dressed and quickly braided her hair before changing into my own work clothes. The two of us brushed our teeth side by side in my bathroom. Soon we were both ready for the day, and as we walked down the hallway to the front door, I checked the clock in the kitchen. Even with the added bath time, we were right on schedule.

As I walked out the front door, my gaze ventured up to the apartment above the garage. I couldn't stop my mind from flashing to the other day at Kate's apartment, when we'd ended up on the kitchen floor. Not that I was complaining.

I'd been surprised that someone as kitchen-savvy as she was would make such a rookie dishwasher mistake . . . but once we wound up having some of the best sex of my life on her kitchen floor? It all made sense. And hey, I wasn't the kind of guy to turn down quickie kitchen sex. I wasn't entirely sure that that elusive male creature even existed. Sex was amazing, no matter the locale.

Blinking away the erotic thoughts, I helped Maddie

into her car seat and fastened myself in the front.

"Let's get you to preschool."

•••

By the time I arrived at the office, a huge pile of paperwork was waiting for me on my desk. Sighing, I sat down and immediately got to work. Bus routes on the west side of town needed reorganizing, train tracks needed maintenance, potholes on the highway needed to be filled . . . and all I could think about was filling Kate.

Focus, Hunter, focus.

Thankfully, the rest of the day went by in a flash, and soon it was time for me to pick Maddie up from her best friend's house. I'd had a feeling that my last meeting of the day would run a little late, so I scheduled a playdate for Maddie with Ashley. Just one of the many skills I'd had to quickly learn as a single dad.

On the car ride home, Maddie asked what we'd be having for dinner, and then whined when I told her we'd be having chicken and broccoli, one of our go-to weekday dinners.

"Why can't you make the same yummy dinner Kate made us when she came over?"

"Neighbor Kate is a much better chef than I am," I replied, checking for Maddie's reaction in the rearview mirror. She didn't look convinced.

"Well, why can't you tell her to come over and cook for us again?"

You have no idea how badly I want to invite her over.

"Kate has helped us out a lot lately. It's been very nice of her, but we don't want to take advantage of her kindness."

"Daddy, what does 'advantage' mean?"

I sighed. "I just mean that we can't expect her to make us dinner all the time. We have to learn to do it ourselves."

Besides, she made it pretty clear a while ago that she wasn't interested in something serious—and the last thing I want to do is use my kid to guilt her into anything.

Maddie was silent for a while, staring out the window from her car seat. A few minutes later, she sighed and muttered to herself, "But I hate broccoli."

•••

I spent all of dinner and all of Maddie's bedtime routine trying to find an excuse to text Kate without sounding completely and hopelessly desperate.

I could ask her for the recipe of that meal she made that Maddie loved so much—but I promised myself I'd stop using my daughter as an excuse. I could check in and make sure her dishwasher was holding up okay—but it was clear that the whole dishwasher fiasco was a ruse, and I didn't want to tease her about it.

By the time I put Maddie to bed, I was completely stumped and ready to just shoot Kate a dumb "hey" text.

As I tucked Maddie in, placing a kiss on her forehead and telling her I loved her, I couldn't help but shake my head at the stupidity of this whole situation. This little princess was the only one who truly mattered in my life. Even if my new tenant was fun, I was a dad first. Maddie and I were a package deal, and long-term, I'd need a woman who understood that.

"Good night, Daddy," Maddie said softly, her eyelids

fluttering closed.

My heart squeezed as I looked down at her small form curled up under the blankets. "Good night, sweetheart. See you in the morning."

I walked to my bedroom and grabbed my phone from the bedside table. Checking the screen, I was surprised to see that I had a text waiting from Kate.

Are you there?

Her text was more direct than usual. Something might be wrong. I called her immediately, worried that she might be in trouble.

"Hello?" she whispered, her voice barely a squeak.

"Kate, hi, is everything okay?" I tried to keep my voice calm and measured. The last thing she needed was to hear me freaked out.

"I, uh, I heard a noise. I think there might be someone . . . or something . . . here. Do you think you could come over and check it out?"

Within a few minutes, I was walking through Kate's unlocked front door and into her darkened apartment. *Maybe I should have grabbed a baseball bat or something.*

"Kate?" I called out, my eyes still adjusting to the darkness.

"Over here," she replied in a loud whisper.

Following her voice, I walked into the living room to find her curled up on the couch under a blanket pulled all the way up to her chin. Her eyes were the size of softballs—and glued to the horror movie playing on the TV. Part of me thought that she looked genuinely freaked out, but after the way she staged the dishwasher disaster before? I wasn't so sure.

"What are you watching?" I asked, my voice neutral. If she was really freaked out, I didn't want to seem like I was making fun of her.

"Well," she said, turning to look at me and widening her eyes even more, "this movie came on TV, and at the beginning it didn't look like it would be scary, it just looked really interesting, so I kept watching, and, uh, well, it really freaked me out, and then I heard a noise on the other side of the apartment, and now here you are."

She said it all at once, her explanation coming out in a fast, steady stream—almost like she'd been rehearsing it for the past ten minutes. I smiled.

"That sounds awful," I said a little sarcastically, grabbing the remote from her coffee table and switching the movie off. "Let's start by getting the screaming and the zombies off your TV."

"Good idea," she said, nodding and shifting under her blanket on the couch.

"Well, I think there's only one thing left to do," I said, tucking my hands into my back pockets.

"What's that?" She furrowed her brow, her eyes still wide.

"I think you'd better come sleep over at my place."

Her eyes grew even wider. "Can we do that?"

"We'll set an alarm so you can sneak out early." *Not that we'll be doing much sleeping.*

"That'll be the shortest walk of shame ever."

"At least there's a good chance no one will see you."

We both laughed.

"Yeah, I think sleeping over would be nice," she said, sitting up and tucking her hair behind her ear.

"Good." I smiled. "Now, get out from under that blanket so we can get out of here before the zombie in your bedroom finds us."

She rolled her eyes but followed me to the door, where she slipped her shoes on.

Kate and I crept quickly and quietly over to my place, tiptoeing past Maddie's room and into mine. Once Kate stepped around me, I closed and locked the door behind us.

Never making that mistake again.

I turned around and Kate wrapped her arms around me, pressing her lips to mine with surprising softness.

"Thanks for rescuing me," she said between kisses, running her hands over my chest and shoulders.

"I'm glad you called." I moved my hands down to her waist. "You never know what kind of crazies are out there."

"Mmm," she murmured as my mouth moved to her neck, gently nibbling the soft skin below her ear. She made a tiny, need-filled sound and pulled at the buttons on my shirt, slowly unfastening them one by one.

While her fingers worked at getting my shirt off, I slid my hands under her top, reaching around to undo the clasp of her bra. We both finished our tasks at the same time, pausing to pull our shirts over our heads and toss them to the floor.

I then guided Kate to the edge of my bed, where I slowly peeled down her black leggings, enjoying each new inch of bare skin on display. Once her pants were off, I quickly shed my jeans. Our eyes locked, we removed our underwear at the same time and stood there for a moment, looking at each other.

"Come here." My voice came out rougher than I intended as I took her hand and tugged her to my chest. The feel of her bare skin against mine was exquisite, and all those ample curves were enough to make my mouth water at the opportunity to explore every inch of her body.

I lifted her into my arms, and Kate responded by locking her ankles around my hips. Her mouth met mine in a hungry kiss as I lowered us onto the bed.

I laid her back, dragging my tongue down her neck and over her breasts, where I paused briefly to suck and tease her nipples as she settled against the pillows. Kate moaned at the feel of my tongue rolling over her skin, making me even more eager to keep moving my mouth farther south. Trailing my lips down her torso, I paused just before I reached my destination, moving instead to her inner thigh.

Kate sighed impatiently and chuckled softly. "You're such a—ooh . . ."

Before she could finish her sentence, I began kissing between her legs, running my tongue over her sensitive flesh. She was even wetter than I thought she would be, and the warmth of her arousal turned me on more.

I continued working my tongue over her pussy, sucking gently on her clit, making her breathe harder and harder. Kate's moans grew more frequent until I sent her over the edge and her orgasm washed over her, causing her back to arch.

When her breathing returned to normal, she propped herself up on her elbows, raising one hand and curling her finger at me. "Come here," she whispered.

Bringing my face close, I aligned my body over hers, lowering myself until I could feel her breasts pressing into my chest.

I was dying to bury myself balls-deep right then, but thankfully still had enough functioning brain cells left to reach for the bedside table and grab a condom. After covering myself in latex, I felt Kate's fist curl around me as she guided me back into position.

Our mouths stayed fused together as I sank into her tight heat. Kate made a wordless sound of pleasure and shifted to accommodate my length. We both sighed as I slowly slid myself inside her, inch by inch. Unable to hold back, even though I wanted to, I pumped my hips and she lifted her hips with each thrust, matching my pace. We were getting good at this—finding the perfect rhythm with each other quickly and easily, both inside and outside the bedroom. Everything with her felt so effortless.

Our breathing quickened. Kate's moans grew more and more frequent, reaching a level of intensity that told me I was going to have to cover her mouth with my hand again. I brought my hand back to her chest, massaging her breast and rolling her nipple between my fingers while she raked her fingernails over my back, occasionally reaching up the back of my neck to gently pull my hair.

"You are . . . amazing," she whispered breathlessly, her back arching again as her second orgasm mounted.

I felt her tighten around me and knew my own release was getting closer. But ladies always came first.

"Come for me," I murmured, and within moments, she inhaled a shaky breath, her entire body trembling. "That's it . . ." I thrust harder, finding the angle that finally made her come apart.

That was all it took for me, watching her unravel in my arms. I twitched inside her, emptying myself into the condom as a powerful orgasm tore through me, making me curse under my breath.

When I opened my eyes, Kate was watching me in

wonder with a small smile on her lips.

Panting, we both lay back on the bed, covered in a thin layer of sweat. Just as I settled into my pillow, Kate turned onto her side, propping her head up on her elbow. I turned to look at her and found a mischievous look on her face, a single eyebrow arched.

"What's that look?" I asked, mirroring her body language and rolling onto my side.

"I think I'm in love with this slumber party."

Chapter Thirteen

Kate

"Cheers to being adults."

Jessie grinned, holding up her margarita. Rebecca had just been promoted at work, Jessie was celebrating her sixth wedding anniversary next week, and I was finally settled in after the move.

The three of us hadn't seen each other for a few weeks, so we'd planned a girls' day complete with manis and pedis, a massage, shopping, and now happy hour at my favorite Mexican restaurant.

It was a warm Saturday and we were sitting on the patio, people watching and catching up. Because I hadn't seen Rebecca or Jessie since I'd moved in, they had no idea what had been going on with Hunter. I'd tried to avoid the conversation because I wasn't exactly sure what to tell them about him, especially since I didn't really understand our relationship myself.

"So, how's birthday-sex guy?" Rebecca asked as if

she could read my thoughts.

My cheeks warmed. God, what was wrong with me? I was like a teenager being asked about her crush. I decided to go on the defensive and try to play it off.

"Let's just say he was worth the wait." I grinned, hoping they wouldn't want too many details.

"Oh my God! You hooked up?" Rebecca exclaimed, her hand over her mouth.

Jessie had stopped in mid-bite of her taco and was gaping at me. "You guys had sex?" she asked incredulously.

"How did you not tell us this earlier?" Rebecca asked, sipping her margarita.

"It just sort of happened . . ." I trailed off. "A few times."

"Oh my God!" Rebecca said again. A group of people passing by on the street turned to stare at us.

"You're causing a scene," I said in a low voice, raising an eyebrow at her. "Can you stop shouting?"

"I can't believe you're having sex with your landlord," Jessie said, then finally took a bite of her taco.

"Well, it sounds bad when you put it that way." I furrowed my eyebrows. "We're friends. Friends who watch movies and occasionally have sex on the floor of my apartment."

"The floor?" Jessie was laughing now.

"That was just one time." I grinned crookedly at the memory. "The rest of the time, we've made it to a bed."

"Hold on a minute." Rebecca put up a hand. "What do you mean, watch movies? You're actually hanging out? Not just hooking up?"

"Kind of. He's fun." I shrugged. "And his daughter is nice."

Jessie and Rebecca exchanged meaningful looks.

"What?" I asked, finishing my margarita. I hadn't come prepared for the third degree, and it was starting to freak me out. Thankfully, the margaritas were strong.

"The daughter who walked in on you? You all hang out now?"

"Look, it's just friendly. It's not a big deal. We're not dating."

Jessie waved the server over to our table. "We need three more, please." She turned back to me. "This is insane. You never like anyone."

"I don't *like* him," I said. "I mean, I do, as a friend. But I told him to date other people."

"Kate!" Rebecca was almost shouting again.

"What?" I asked, exasperated. I didn't like that they were pushing me on this. Two people could hang out and like each other without dating, which was what Hunter and I were doing.

"You finally like someone, and you tell him to date other people?" Jessie asked.

"Look, we said from the beginning that it's just casual. You know me." I accepted another drink from our server gratefully. "I'm not looking for something serious."

Jessie gave me a curious look. "But what do you really want from this?"

What did I want? A few orgasms? I could barely

answer that question myself, never mind explain what I was feeling to my friends.

"How'd you get his daughter to like you?" Rebecca raised her eyebrows at me. "Last I heard, she'd chased you out of their house."

"I made them dinner and helped out with this bake sale," I said, taking another large sip of my margarita. "She warmed up to me." I paused. "But she doesn't know her dad and I are hooking up, which might change the way she feels."

Jessie and Rebecca exchanged glances again.

"Can you two please stop doing that?" I asked.

Rebecca put her hand on mine. "I hate to break it to you, Kate, but it sounds like you and Hunter are dating. Or at the very least, have feelings for each other."

I pulled my hand away and crossed my arms. "Come on, we're just casual."

"It's okay to date someone," Jessie said, leaning on an elbow. "It doesn't have to be scary. It's just what you've been doing. Cooking, watching movies, hanging out. That's all dating is."

Rebecca nodded. "We love you and think you're amazing, and just want you to be happy. And it sounds like Hunter does make you happy. Why not just go for it?"

I'd thought talking to my friends would help clarify things for me, but it had only made everything more complicated. I didn't date people; it just wasn't who I was. I didn't like commitment.

Hunter and I were having fun now, but what would happen a few years down the road when the fun wore off and reality set in? I'd end up just like my sister, in a bitter divorce. She'd been in love once too. She and her ex had seemed like the perfect couple, and now they couldn't even be in the same room together. And our parents didn't have a great relationship, either. After barely tolerating each other for many years, they finally divorced when we were teens.

This was exactly what I'd spent my life trying to avoid. I hated the idea of loving someone, pouring everything into a relationship and then having it all go wrong.

Several margaritas later, Rebecca and I shared a cab home from the restaurant. As I stared out the window, I slipped deep into thought about the situation with Hunter.

"Look, I know this stuff freaks you out, but dating is fun. Seriously, being married is fun." She interrupted my thoughts, patting my shoulder. "Aren't you sick of going out on bad dates and having disappointing sex?"

I shrugged. I hadn't really thought about it before, but after meeting Hunter, the idea of hooking up with someone else held no interest. I knew I was in denial. I liked Hunter, but I didn't know how to navigate this situation. Usually when things got complicated, I checked out. But rather than wanting to avoid him, I found myself wishing I could see him.

When the cab stopped in front of Hunter's house, Rebecca gave me a sympathetic pat on the knee. "I know you'll figure it out." She smiled.

"Thanks, *Mom*." I laughed, climbing out of the car. I paused and turned back to her. "But seriously, you're the best."

I leaned over the seat to give her a quick hug and

watched the cab drive down the block. Once I was inside, I changed into sweatpants and a cozy T-shirt and lay back on my bed.

After a few minutes of deliberation, and a little liquid courage thanks to that last margarita, I decided to text Hunter.

Hey, want to watch a movie at my place?

I paced the apartment, waiting for his response, and glanced out the window. His bedroom light was on, so that was a good sign. My phone pinged that he'd replied, and I pounced on it.

I'm actually going on a date, with the woman from the bake sale. Maybe tomorrow?

I stared at my phone, my heart pounding inside my chest. I tossed the phone aside and put my hands over my face, falling back onto the bed, almost sick to my stomach at the thought.

What was I doing? This was insane. I was the one who'd encouraged him to go on a date. I had no right to be upset . . . but I was. I didn't want him to date other people, but how could I say that to him? *I don't want to be in a relationship, but I also don't want you to start a relationship with anyone else.* He'd think I was ridiculous, which I was.

I pulled a pillow over my face and screamed as I tried not to picture Hunter on his date.

Chapter Fourteen

Hunter

"More wine, sir?" the waiter asked, mercifully interrupting what was quickly becoming the worst date I'd ever been on in my entire life. The charming Italian place used to be one of my favorite restaurants, the perfect blend of classy and not too formal, presumably an excellent choice for a first date. But in this moment? I wanted to leave and never come back.

"Yes, please, that would be great," I said, trying to ignore the fact that June had spent the past half hour either droning on about her daughter's bowel problems, or throwing back glass after glass of white wine. I think we were on number six, and I was starting to think I should get drunk myself to make it through the rest of this disaster.

"You are quickly becoming my *favorite* waiter," June purred, poking the scared-looking young man in the arm. Apparently, she was a little tipsier than she realized and poked him harder than she meant to, causing him to spill some wine on the white tablecloth.

"My apologies," the waiter said, clearly panicked, pulling a towel from his apron pocket and dabbing at the spot.

"Whoopsies!" June giggled and took another long sip of her wine.

"No, we're sorry. Don't worry about it, thank you." I gave the waiter an apologetic look and waved him off. With a worried nod, he finished dabbing the spot on the table and hurried away.

June turned her attention to me. "So, what about you? Have you given Maddie's grade school any thought? I mean, clearly your mind was in the right place with preschool. Too many parents overlook it as the foundation of a good education, but I think that sometimes it's easy to forget how important the next steps can be . . ."

Apparently, I'd completely tuned out the last part of our conversation, and we had somehow skipped from poo to elementary school.

I opened my mouth to respond but June went on,

something about the importance of setting up our children for success as early as possible. Involuntarily, I slowly started to tune her out again. I agreed with what she was saying for the most part, but we'd been talking about our kids for so long, I was beginning to think they were the only thing we had in common.

"I don't know. What do you think? Hunter?" June was looking expectantly at me, her eyebrows practically touching her hairline.

"I'm sorry. I must have spaced out for a moment. What were you saying?"

In any other situation, I would have made up an excuse, but at that point, I didn't really care about saving face. She was plastered, and I was miserable. No point in pretending this was anything other than what it was, right?

"I was just wondering what you think about choosing public or private schools. But then there are charter schools, boarding schools . . . there are just so many choices."

"Honestly, I haven't given it too much thought yet. I'm just trying to hang in there with the day-to-day stuff.

We've just now got a handle on preschool," I replied, doing my best to sound normal and engaged. *If Kate were the one sitting across from me right now, I guarantee I'd be having way more fun right now.*

"Ugh, you're so right. This single-parent thing is no joke." She nodded, leaning toward me with her elbows on the table. "You know I'm always here if you need anything."

"I appreciate that, June. We've been managing so far."

She nodded again, slowly raising a single eyebrow. "I suppose you already have some extra help. I remember from the bake sale. Kara, was it?"

Here we go.

"Kate," I said coolly. *Let the grilling begin.*

"Kate, right. That was awfully sweet of her to bake that pie for you two. Have your tenants always been so helpful and . . . involved?"

"Kate's special, that's for sure," I heard myself saying.

June's eyebrow arched even higher. It was clear she was trying to make her interest seem as innocent as possible, but I could tell from the look on her face that she was suspicious. And honestly, she had every reason to be. Not that I was about to let her know that. Single dad with a fuck buddy wasn't exactly the reputation I'd been going for among the other preschool parents.

"Kate's turned out to be such a huge help," I added, putting my best stressed-out parent look on my face. "And Maddie has really taken to her." *Not to mention Kate's funny, brilliant, confident, sexy—pretty much everything I could ever want in a partner.*

"How special for you and Maddie," June said, her voice almost too sweet. "I might have to steal her from you. I'm always looking for better help." She winked, clearly misunderstanding the nature of Kate's help. But hey, I wasn't about to correct her.

I smiled weakly and took a sip of my wine. Before June could grill me any further about Kate, the waiter arrived with our meals. As he placed my entrée in front of me, the smell of the fennel and perfectly browned butter wafted up from the plate, melting away all my frustrations with June.

Who cared if I was on a stupid date with a woman who only wanted to talk about the schools our children would go to? Who cared if she ordered a Caesar salad at a restaurant famous for their handmade pasta? I had my sausage and my pasta, and in that moment, that was all that mattered.

If Kate were here, she would have ordered something interesting, like the pumpkin ravioli or the eggplant parmesan. She would have let me try some of her food, and I would have rocked her world with this house-made sausage . . . before rocking her world with my own sausage later.

Okay, maybe my food wasn't the only thing that mattered.

As the date went on, June managed to become even more boring. When she'd completely exhausted the topic of our kids' schools, she moved on to her new favorite movie that she'd just seen last week.

"I'm a sucker for any movie about horses," she said, pushing a crouton around her plate. "Put a horse in a movie, and I'm there. Have you seen *War Horse*? If you haven't, you have to. Immediately. It's *amazing*."

I nodded, stuffing a huge bite of sausage into my mouth so it was clear I couldn't politely respond. I'd never seen a movie about horses in my life, and I wasn't looking to start anytime soon.

"What's the last movie you saw?" June asked, batting her lashes.

My mind immediately traveled to the last time I saw Kate, when she was curled up on the couch pretending to be freaked out by a scary movie. It was probably the most creative booty call I'd ever received in my life . . . but a booty call, nonetheless. And not really the kind of thing you mention on a first date, no matter how horribly it's going.

"Probably something with princesses or talking animals," I said, leaning back in my chair. "I don't really have time for adult movies these days."

"Adult movies?" A sly grin spread across June's face.

Shit.

"No—not like that. I'm not really a porn guy. Not

that there's anything wrong with watching those kinds of films, necessarily, I just, uh, no. But yeah, that's not what I meant. I meant movies not made for children."

I didn't know why I was rambling so much. Who cared what this woman thought? Not me, that was for sure. But the last thing I needed was for her to report back to the other parents at our school that I was a porn addict. Not the best look for me. More importantly, it wouldn't bode well for Maddie.

Jesus, I just want this night to be over with.

"Mmm, don't worry, I understand." June raised her wineglass and gave me a knowing wink.

Great. Guess I can add local perv to the list of things I'm known for with the preschool parents.

I laughed awkwardly, racking my brain for something to say to change the subject. Before I could come up with anything, the waiter returned to check on us, asking if we'd like to see a dessert menu after eyeing our almost-empty plates.

For the love of God, let this date end before dessert.

"Not tonight," June said to the waiter, crinkling her nose in disappointment. He nodded politely and cleared our plates. "Sorry for deciding for you. My babysitter just texted that she needs me."

"No worries. I should get back too," I replied, grateful to be wrapping things up. "Is everything okay?"

"Oh yeah, everything's fine," she insisted. "The babysitter just has a, uh . . . math test or something tomorrow. That's what I get for hiring the high schooler next door."

If I didn't know any better, I would have guessed that June was the one bailing on me. *Guess I'm not the only one having a bad time on this date after all.*

When the waiter returned with our check, I insisted on paying. My values might have been archaic, but letting the woman pay for the first date didn't sit right with me. *Kate would kill me if she heard me say that out loud.*

After finishing our wine, June and I walked to the parking lot together, where I waited until her cab pulled up, and then we shared an uncomfortable side hug. She wore too much perfume, which I found overpowering. It was nothing like Kate's subtle scent.

Once the cab drove off, I made my way to my car. I hadn't realized that she took a cab to the restaurant, and suddenly it made sense why she drank so much wine. She was probably a little nervous that I'd finally said yes to her standing dinner-date invitation. And besides, what single parent wouldn't want to let a little loose every once in a while, even if that only meant having an extra couple of glasses of wine with dinner?

On the drive home, I went over all the times I thought about Kate during dinner. It felt a little unfair to June for me to be so checked out during the time I was supposed to be getting to know her, but I couldn't help it. Every time I thought about what I wanted in a woman, Kate immediately popped into my head. Casual, no-strings-attached sex might be every man's wet dream, but with the way things were going, it was suddenly starting to seem like a really bad idea.

Maybe it was because of Maddie. Of course I wanted a female role model for her, and I wanted her to experience a mother's love.

Sure, there were parenting books and internet articles

that could walk me through all the right things to say to my daughter as she "embarked on her journey into womanhood." But in the back of my mind, I had a feeling all that would mean a lot more coming from someone who knew what it was like, who'd experienced it firsthand. Someone who loved my daughter as much as I did. And as much as it sucked, that woman would most likely not be Kate. Bridging the gap from booty call to stepmom was a big leap, and I couldn't afford to let myself or Maddie become emotionally connected with Kate if she wasn't going to stick around.

When I pulled into the driveway, I glanced up at Kate's window over the garage. The light was off, which either meant she was out or she'd called it an early night. Either way, my heart sank a little, knowing that I couldn't head over to her place for a few minutes to tell her about my horrible date.

I walked inside, paying and thanking the babysitter before walking her to the front door. Maddie had been asleep for about an hour by then, and I didn't want to wake her by saying good night.

As I changed into sweats, kicking my dark jeans into

the laundry hamper, it dawned on me. All these thoughts about Kate didn't have to do with Maddie. Not completely, at least.

It was me. I was the one who needed another person around, someone who could fill in the gaps I struggled with in my life, who was there at the end of the day to support me, who was funny and brilliant and sexy as hell, a true partner.

I sat on the edge of my bed, burying my face in my palms and rubbing my eyes. The only problem with these newfound feelings was that Kate didn't want anything to do with them. She made it perfectly clear, right from the beginning, that she wasn't looking for anything serious, especially with someone who had a kid. Catching feelings, she called it.

Fuck, fuck, fuck.

For as much as I wished Kate wanted something more than just being fuck buddies, I didn't want to be the kind of guy who agreed to casual sex and then freaked out after a few hot-and-heavy nights. We'd agreed this would be nothing serious. I had to honor that arrangement.

But I had to do something about these feelings. And fast.

Chapter Fifteen

Kate

"Dirty martini, please," I shouted to the bartender over the noise of the crowd.

It was a Wednesday night, and I'd been sent to an album release party for an up-and-coming singer. According to my editor, there would be major gossip to pick up at the party, but so far all I'd done was eat too many fried goat-cheese balls and listen to bad pop music for an hour. The singer was only eighteen, and I'd already had to dodge groups of drunk teenagers on more than one occasion. I decided a drink was necessary to get me through the rest of the night.

I sipped my martini as I walked through the party. My mind wandered to Hunter, and I wondered what he was doing. The last we'd spoken, he'd been getting ready for a date with that bitch from Maddie's school.

Okay, she wasn't a bitch. But I hated the thought of him out with her. And while I was dying to know how it had gone, I wasn't about to ask Hunter about it. I refused to seem like a needy girlfriend, especially because we weren't dating, and even more so because I was the one who'd encouraged him to go on the date in the first place.

Someone tapped me on the shoulder, interrupting my thoughts.

"Hey, gorgeous," a voice said as I turned around. It was Andy, a fellow columnist.

I winced at the greeting. We'd hooked up a few times, usually after drinking too much at these events. He was attractive and fun to hang out with, but I hated when he called me pet names.

"Hey, Andy." I smiled as he pulled me in for a hug.

"I haven't seen you in a while." He grinned, his gaze lingering on my cleavage for a moment too long. "You look great."

We filled each other in on our lives after Andy bought us another round of martinis. Usually, I was happy to see him—he was fun and easy to be around—but tonight our conversation felt stale. I wasn't in the mood to flirt with him, and I certainly wasn't in the mood to go home with him. In fact, the more I talked to Andy, the more I missed Hunter.

Shit. I was really in deep.

I told Andy I had to use the restroom, but really, I just wanted to be alone with my thoughts for a few minutes.

Lately, I'd been doing a lot of thinking about relationships. All this time, I'd thought that by avoiding a relationship I was being strong and independent, but in reality, I was just afraid to grow up. I was too old to be at this party, and I was too old to keep being afraid to live my life. It was time to make adult decisions and take a risk. Yes, I'd seen my sister get burned, but that didn't mean I would. And if I did, I'd pick myself back up. That's what a truly strong and independent woman would do.

I looked at myself in the bathroom mirror. For so many years, I'd been missing out on having a real connection with someone because I was afraid. But now I was ready.

Excited by my new realization, I smiled to myself. As I left the bathroom, I took a sip of my martini and looked through the party again, hoping to spot a budding romance between the pop star and one of the partygoers, or even maybe a fight. I hated to leave without any takeaways for my column.

Before I could find anything, my phone vibrated in my pocket. I pulled it out and answered. "Hello?"

"Kate, hey, it's Hunter." He sounded frantic, and I couldn't hear the rest of what he said over the noises of the party.

"Whoa, slow down," I said, quickly stepping out onto the balcony where a group of models were smoking. "What happened?"

"Maddie's in the hospital."

My heart sank, and I put a hand over my mouth in shock.

"Is she okay?" I asked, already heading for the door.

"I'm not sure yet. We just got here, and the doctors are taking a look." His voice sounded close to breaking. "I guess I just wanted to let you know."

"I'm coming," I said as I stepped out the front doors.

"It's okay, it sounds like you're out. You don't have to," he said, but I cut him off.

"Hunter, I'm already on my way. I'll be there soon."

•••

I got to the hospital in record time and practically flew up the stairs. When I spotted Hunter in the waiting area, I ran up to him.

"How is she?" I asked, trying to catch my breath.

"She's in surgery," he said, worry etched on his face. "It's her appendix. They said it's a simple procedure and that it's nothing to worry about."

I could tell that he wasn't convinced. I could only imagine how it felt as a parent to have your child in surgery.

I threw my arms around him and held him tight. He wrapped his arms around me as I rested my head against his chest. It felt so comfortable to lean on him like that, so much so that I lingered, not wanting the moment to end.

"She'll be fine," I said, pulling back to meet his eyes. I hated the pain and anguish I saw reflected in them. "I had the same surgery when I was her age."

"Thanks for coming." He reached out to brush a stray hair from my face.

We moved into the waiting room and sat in the hard plastic chairs.

"Of course I came. I didn't want you to be here alone."

He looked into my eyes, and my heart sped up. Now wasn't the time to tell him what I'd realized, but being here for him felt really good.

"Have you eaten anything?" I asked, glancing at my watch. It was almost nine.

"No, actually." He ran a hand along the back of his neck. "I totally forgot about it."

I stood up. "Let me go grab you something."

"No, you don't have to," he said, but I held up a hand.

"Please, it's the least I can do."

He smiled as I grabbed my purse and headed out the

doors. Ten minutes later, I was back with a sandwich and some fruit from the hospital cafeteria.

"Any news?" I asked as I set down the bag.

"She's out of surgery," he said, smiling. "She's fine, just recovering, and I can go see her in a bit."

I let out a sigh of relief and smiled back. "Thank God. I haven't been that scared in a while."

"Having you here meant a lot," he said as I handed him the bag. "Sorry if I interrupted your date."

Confused, I stared at him for a moment, then shook my head. "Oh no, it wasn't a date. It was a stupid work party."

He nodded, and I could see the relief on his face.

I stared at him for a moment before smiling to myself. The realization that Hunter was jealous caused a fluttering in my stomach.

"I'm glad you called me," I added, unable to hold back my grin. I wanted to tell him how important it was to me to be here for him and Maddie, to be included in moments like this, but I didn't know how to say it.

Instead, I gave him another hug and melted into the feel of his arms wrapped around me.

We were interrupted by the doctor approaching.

"Maddie's parents?" the doctor asked.

Hunter rose to his feet. "Just me."

I stood by his side, our fingers clasped together tightly as the doctor dismissed me and looked directly at Hunter with concern in her eyes. "Maddie's awake now. She did very well. Visitation is for family only if you want to go see her now." She motioned down the hallway.

Hunter turned to me. "Thanks again. I'm probably going to stay the night while Maddie recovers."

"Yeah, of course." I nodded. "I'll keep watch at the house."

I smiled, but my heart was sinking. I didn't want to leave without them and go home to an empty house. I gave Hunter's hand a final squeeze before heading out.

As I pulled in the driveway, the house looked huge and menacing in the dark without any lights on. Usually when I pulled in, I could see Maddie watching TV or playing a game in the living room window. I was struck by a pang of loneliness as I got out of my car and walked to my apartment. I'd gotten so used to having them around that I hadn't realized how it might feel when they were gone.

Once I was inside, I lay down on my bed, staring up at the ceiling. My phone rang, and hoping it was Hunter, I answered it quickly without looking at the caller ID.

"Hunter?" I said into the phone without thinking.

"Who's Hunter?" It was my sister, Kayla.

"Sorry—nobody. How are you?"

Between moving and everything happening with Hunter, I hadn't talked to Kayla in a couple of weeks.

"Good," she said, drawing out the word. I hadn't heard her sound this cheerful in a long time.

"What's with you?" I asked. "You sound giddy."

She laughed. "Can't I just be happy?"

I bit my lip. I didn't want to say it, but I didn't think I'd seen her happy since before her divorce.

"All right, fine," she said before I had to answer. "I met someone."

I sat up in bed, my eyes wide. It was the second surprising phone call I'd had that night. "What? Tell me everything."

"Kate, he's amazing," she said, practically swooning over the phone. "His name is Tyler. He's so sweet and caring and helpful. Everything Jim wasn't, basically."

"What do you mean?" I'd always thought she and Jim seemed like a great couple. Honestly, I'd never really understood why they didn't work out. "I thought Jim was all of those things."

She sighed. "Look, Kate, there's a lot I didn't tell you about Jim and me. There were problems from the start that I didn't want to admit. I pretended we were this perfect couple so nobody would notice that we weren't that great for each other."

I was floored. I'd never heard her talk this way before about Jim. He'd always seemed nice at family events, but I guess I'd never really known him that well.

"So, you think things are different now? With Tyler?"

"Absolutely. Seriously, I've never felt this way before. I know it sounds crazy, but he's such a great person, and he understands me."

I could tell she meant it. Looking back on it, I realized she'd never said things like this about Jim. I'd just assumed everything was great because they always seemed happy enough.

Kayla interrupted my thoughts. "I think I love him, Kate."

"Wow, that's amazing," I said, wandering over to the window. I automatically glanced at Hunter's window before remembering that he wasn't there. "Seriously, I'm really happy for you."

We caught up more on everything that had happened with her and Tyler before I told her I had to get to bed.

After I hung up the phone, I curled back up on the bed. I truly was happy for Kayla. After everything she'd gone through with Jim, she deserved to find someone else. And if after her divorce she was brave enough to try again, then I really didn't have an excuse to be afraid.

I didn't know how, but I needed to find a way to let

Hunter know how I was feeling. I just hoped it wasn't too late.

Chapter Sixteen

Hunter

I opened the freezer door and pulled out the yellow box of Popsicles, rifling through the packages to find the right flavor. Maddie had been home from the hospital for a few days, and I learned pretty quickly which colors she preferred. She wasn't a huge fan of the grape ones and she absolutely hated the green lime ones, but everything else she got down just fine.

My gaze landed on a Popsicle that looked like it might be red, so I pulled it out of the box and held it up to the light. Through the thin packaging, I could see a faint red tint. *Hallelujah.* Red was Maddie's favorite.

I walked into the living room where she was curled up under a thick, fuzzy blanket on the couch, still dressed in her pajamas and her hair a little tousled. I unwrapped the Popsicle and handed it to her, making sure to place a napkin in her lap.

"Be careful that it doesn't start dripping," I said, brushing her hair behind her ear.

"I know," she said softly, nodding without taking her eyes away from the TV. She absentmindedly pulled the frozen treat toward her mouth, missing on her first try and smearing red juice on her chin.

Taking the napkin from her lap, I wiped the juice away, chuckling at how unfazed she seemed. The doctors had warned me that she would need lots of rest after the surgery, but that morning, I could tell she'd turned a corner by how entranced she was with her cartoons. Her first couple of days home, she could barely keep her eyes open long enough to pay attention to them. But now, she was hooked. I could already tell I'd have to be firm about getting her back to her normal screen-time schedule once she was fully recovered.

"I'll get you another napkin," I said, kissing the top of Maddie's head before walking back into the kitchen.

Turns out, there was nothing more terrifying in the world than having to take your child to the hospital. I learned that the hard way. Even after the doctors reassured me that she'd be fine and that her surgery was totally routine and manageable, I couldn't deal with how helpless I'd felt.

Sitting in that waiting room while strangers cut open my daughter with nothing to do but sit and wait and try not to freak out? I'd thought I was a calm and rational person, but based on the chaotic feelings that churned through me during that time, I was starting to question everything I thought I knew about myself. The only thing I didn't question? The fact that Maddie meant everything to me. She was my whole world, and it was my job to make sure nothing bad ever happened to her. Case closed.

After grabbing a fresh napkin, I walked back into the living room and sat down next to her on the couch. I placed the napkin in her lap, smiling at the fact that her Popsicle was already halfway gone.

"Daddy, can we have something other than soup for dinner tonight?" Maddie asked, still staring straight ahead at the TV.

"What do you want instead?" I did a mental inventory, trying to remember what groceries we still had. I'd been doing my best to make mild and nutritious meals with what we already had on hand.

"Could we make gluten-free pizza?" She looked up at me with wide, hopeful eyes.

I smiled. Looked like someone was starting to feel better after all.

•••

A few days later, it was clear that Maddie and I needed to get out of the house. We had run out of Popsicles, and our pantry desperately needed to be restocked. And for as much as she and I loved spending time together, I could tell she was ready to look at someone else's face and listen to someone else's voice for a while. And I knew just who to call.

After a few rings, the line connected, and a voice I hadn't realized just how much I missed answered.

"Hunter, hi. How's Maddie doing?"

"Hi, Kate. She's doing a lot better. Thanks for asking." I couldn't keep myself from smiling into my cell phone. Damn, I'd missed the sound of her voice.

"Is her incision healing okay? No signs of infection? No weird side effects from the anesthesia?"

"You've been stress-googling, haven't you?"

We both laughed.

"Listen," she said, her tone turning serious, "this is the first surgery in my life in a long time, and it turns out there's a lot to worry about with these things. Hospitals are rife with infections and all sorts of other things you can catch."

I smiled. *How is it that Kate just gets better and better every time we talk?*

"Well, it's very sweet of you to worry, but she's doing fine."

"Good, I'm glad to hear it. It took just about every ounce of self-control I had to keep myself from texting you every five seconds."

"You can always text me, Kate. You know that, right?"

She paused, and I worried for a second that I'd said too much.

Whatever, it's true. Our physical arrangement might have been a casual one, but rushing to the hospital to help when my daughter had to have emergency surgery? Not exactly what you'd expect from a casual hookup.

"I know, I just—I didn't want to overstep."

"I understand," I said slowly. "But just for the record, you wouldn't have been overstepping. Not in the slightest."

A longer silence stretched between us, and I really started to worry that I'd freaked her out.

"Kate? You still there?"

"Sorry, yes, I'm here." Her voice sounded smaller, more timid than usual. "That was just . . . sweet, Hunter."

"It's true. So, listen, I was calling to see if you wanted to join Maddie and me on a short trip to the park this afternoon. We're going a little stir-crazy over here. Plus, she would love to see you." I had to lighten the mood before Kate hung up and wrote me off as the clingy idiot who didn't know how to keep a relationship with a woman casual.

"I would love to," she replied. "When are you planning to leave?"

"How does three work for you?"

"Three sounds perfect. Meet you at your front door

then."

"Looking forward to it."

After we hung up, I went to tell Maddie the good news. "Guess what?" I asked, walking into the living room and standing next to the TV.

"What?"

"You and I are going to the park later today. And I just got off the phone with our neighbor Kate, and she said she would come with us."

"Really?" Maddie turned to look at me, her eyes wide and her eyebrows raised. It was really starting to melt my heart how much she enjoyed spending time with Kate.

"Really."

"Yay!" she cried, bouncing in her seat on the couch and kicking her legs in excitement underneath the blanket.

"You know what that means, don't you?" I asked, placing my hands on my hips.

She shook her head.

"It's time for you to change out of those pajamas."

Maddie and I spent the next couple of hours tidying up the living room and getting ready for the park, making sure to keep her incision site clean and protected. She seemed excited to put some real clothes on, and when I helped her tie her tennis shoes, I could tell from the look on her face that she was ready to play outside.

At three o'clock on the dot, Kate knocked on our front door. I went to answer it with Maddie trailing close behind, and the moment I opened the door, Maddie reached out to wrap her arms around Kate's waist.

"Oh, hi there," Kate said, clearly touched by the hug. She looked at me and smiled, her eyes widening.

"I'm feeling a lot better," Maddie said, letting go of Kate and stepping back to look up at her. "I ate a *lot* of Popsicles."

"Popsicles, really? Mmm, I'm jealous. I haven't had one of those in a *long* time," Kate replied, shaking her head.

As the two of them chatted in the doorway, I slung the backpack I'd packed over my shoulder that held the supplies to clean Maddie's incision—just in case we needed them—as well as a couple of waters, an extra jacket in case she got cold, and a couple of granola bars in case she got hungry. I knew I was overreacting a little, but hey, I was still recovering from her surgery too.

Maddie and Kate continued chatting during the whole car ride over to the park, with Maddie explaining what the hospital was like and exactly what it felt like when she woke up. I loved hearing how animated she got talking about this whole experience and appreciated how intently Kate listened and followed along. I'd been worried that Maddie might have been a little traumatized by the whole thing, but she was bouncing back even faster than I'd hoped—both physically and emotionally.

At the park, Maddie led Kate and me to her favorite playground, where she quickly found another little girl her age to play with and tell her hospital story to. Kate and I watched the two of them chatter and giggle for a while before they climbed to the top of the slide, where they huddled together and giggled some more.

I called out to Maddie to remember to take it easy—no running or jumping since she was still healing.

"I forgot how easy it is to make friends at that age,"

Kate said with a smile, crossing her arms over her chest.

"It feels good to get some fresh air." I sighed and stretched out my arms. "I feel like I haven't talked to an adult in months."

"Well, that's not quite true," Kate said, rubbing her arm. "How was your date?"

I paused. "Date?"

Kate dipped her chin and gave me an incredulous look. "With June?"

Shit. "Oh, right. My date with June. God, does the fact that I completely forgot about it make me a total asshole?"

"Only half an asshole, I think." Kate laughed. Maybe it was just wishful thinking, but I could have sworn she looked a little relieved.

"I'll take it." I looked over at her with a half grin. "Well, the date wasn't great, if that wasn't already clear." I chuckled, running my hand over the back of my neck.

"What happened?"

"She didn't do anything wrong. We just didn't really have anything in common besides our kids."

Kate tilted her head, giving me a sidelong look. "That seems like a pretty big thing to have in common to me."

"You'd think it would help, wouldn't you?" I smiled wryly back at her. "But it turns out, sticking two single parents at the same dinner table isn't a surefire recipe for romance."

"I'm not sure that recipe exists," she said, looking down at her feet.

"Maybe not, but I did figure one thing out on that date."

"What's that?"

"That I missed you."

Kate paused then, looking at me with wide, stunned eyes, clearly taken aback. "Hunter . . ."

"Don't worry, I know. I'm not trying to push you into a relationship. What we have is casual. Strictly physical. It's just . . . I would be lying if I said that my shitty date didn't make me wish you were the one I'd had a nice dinner with. Not June."

"It's not that I don't—"

"Really, you don't have to explain. I'm not asking you for anything more. It's just that sometimes I wish we wanted the same thing. But I'm not that guy. You made it clear what you want. I just need to accept that. It's on me."

Kate opened her mouth to speak, but before she could get any words out, Maddie came bounding back up to us with a surprising amount of energy.

"Daddy, can I have a snack?" she asked, grabbing my hand and pulling it toward her.

"Sure, just give me one sec."

I pulled a granola bar out of the backpack and handed it to her. She quickly unwrapped it and took a huge bite. When I checked my watch, it made sense why she was so hungry. It was four thirty, her normal pre-dinner Popsicle time.

I really need to get her back onto our normal routine.

"Are you feeling tired at all, Maddie?" I asked.

“I’m not tired,” she said, scrunching her brows together and looking up at me with a stubborn look on her face.

“Okay, you can play for a little while longer,” I replied.

Maddie scampered off then to get her turn on the swing with her new friend.

“Has work been understanding of everything that’s been going on?” Kate asked.

I smiled, suddenly grateful for her merciful change of subject. We continued chatting for the rest of our time at the park and during the whole car ride back to the house. Everything seemed to be back to normal by then, and I silently hoped that she’d let my small confession go for good.

It’s not that I regretted telling Kate how I felt. I did wish that we wanted the same things. But she made it clear from the beginning what she wanted, and that didn’t include long-term commitment or a kid.

No matter how I was starting to feel, or what I wanted, one thing was clear.

I needed to get over it.

Chapter Seventeen

Kate

What are you two doing today?

I waited for Hunter to reply as I googled fun things to do in the city. I needed to let him know how I felt, and since communication wasn't exactly my strong suit, I decided to show him instead of telling him. I was ready for all of it—the relationship, the commitment, even trying on motherhood. And what better way to show that than to plan a fun day date with him and Maddie?

We're just hanging out today. What's up?

Meet me out front in thirty. I have an idea.

I grinned as I got ready, pulling on a light summer dress that was both flattering and family appropriate.

After much deliberation, I'd decided to take them to the zoo. There was a special exhibit with baby foxes that I'd been hearing about, and I thought it would be cute for Maddie to see them. I knew how much she had loved seeing dinosaur skeletons, and I hoped she'd be just as excited to see animals that were still alive.

I waited out front, nervously tapping my foot, hoping I wasn't being too spontaneous by hijacking their whole day. I mentally slapped myself. Where was my confidence? The day was going to be great.

All my doubts flew from my head as Hunter emerged from the house in a black T-shirt and jeans. He looked as sexy as always, and I had to resist giving him a kiss hello. Maddie ran out from behind him, wearing a pink skirt with a gray T-shirt that said POW! in big white letters.

"Cool outfit," I said, grinning. It was perfect for her.

"Thanks." She smiled, slipping on a pair of black sunglasses.

I held back a laugh, glancing at Hunter. His expressive brown eyes lit up with a smile that sent my heart spiraling.

"Hey," I said, shielding my eyes from the sun. "Thanks for going along with my spontaneity."

"We can always use some excitement." He grinned back at me.

His eyes traced up and down my body, taking in my dress. My breath caught as his gaze paused for a moment at my breasts, which were pressing against the thin material. I felt my nipples harden and hoped he wouldn't notice. My gaze lingered on him for a few seconds before I realized Maddie was looking between us.

"Okay," I said quickly, tearing my gaze from Hunter. "So, are you guys ready to go on an adventure?" I started for my car when Hunter shook his head and guided us to his instead.

"Car seat," he said.

Ah. Right. I guess I had a lot to learn.

I climbed in, and he opened the door to the backseat as Maddie got inside.

"Where are we going?" she asked suspiciously.

"It's a surprise. But I promise it'll be fun."

Hunter strapped Maddie into the backseat before settling into the front.

As we got closer to the zoo, I glanced back and saw Maddie leaning against the window, trying to figure out where we were. When we turned the corner, she gasped.

"Are we seeing the foxes?"

"How did you know about that exhibit?" I asked, raising an eyebrow at Hunter.

"Everyone knows about it," she exclaimed.

I laughed, so relieved she was excited about it that I didn't even care that the surprise was ruined.

When we entered the zoo, Maddie practically sprinted off for the fox exhibit. We looked through the glass at the little foxes, their big ears sticking up.

"Do you like them?" I asked Maddie, who was pressing her face against the glass and waving at them.

"They're so cool," she said, not taking her eyes off them.

"Do you want to play with one?"

She turned to me with her mouth open, apparently speechless.

"I bought a special ticket so you can hold one," I told her, pulling the ticket out of my bag. Her eyes went wide, and she looked at Hunter.

He put his hands up. "Don't look at me. This was all Kate."

He grinned at me as Maddie gaped.

"Come on. Let's go." I motioned toward the ticket desk.

The zoo workers led us into a special room. Maddie was so excited, she was bouncing up and down in anticipation, and in that moment I felt pretty damn proud of myself. When they finally brought the baby fox in, Maddie let out a little shriek. I grinned at Hunter as she held out a tentative hand to pet its soft fur.

Hunter's hand pressed against my lower back. "This is pretty amazing. Thanks for putting this together."

"My pleasure. I'm having fun."

"Not as much fun as her," he said, nodding toward

Maddie, who was squealing with excitement as the little animal licked her hand.

"Nobody has ever had that much fun." I laughed, pulling out my phone to get a picture.

When she was finished, Maddie came bounding over to us and wrapped her arms around my waist, telling me that was the best day she'd ever had.

Shocked, I hugged her back. I'd known she was excited, but I hadn't expected this. Unexpected tears sprang to my eyes, and I quickly blinked them away. *Get a grip, Kate.* Apparently, I'd turned into a huge softie.

As we walked through the zoo, I couldn't keep the smile off my face. Spending time with Hunter and Maddie was even more fun than I'd expected. It felt so natural to be with them like this, and I couldn't help but imagine us doing this kind of thing every weekend.

We came to the big-cats exhibit, where the lion had just had a cub. A huge crowd had gathered in front of the exhibit, and when we finally made our way to the front, we could see the mother lion with her baby.

"That's the dad," I said, pointing to the male lion that

was sunning himself nearby.

I watched Maddie as she leaned against the railing, and all this talk of babies and moms and dads made a question spring to mind. *Do the people around us think I'm Maddie's mom?*

My stomach did a little flip at the thought, and I realized I'd been secretly hoping that's what they thought. Normally I wasn't such a bundle of emotions, but the idea of the three of us being a family made me feel all warm and fuzzy inside. The idea of belonging—of being part of my own personal tribe—sounded better than I ever thought it would.

I watched Hunter as he crouched down and recited lion facts for Maddie. His dark hair had grown a little longer since I'd first met him, and he had a shadow of facial hair dusting his strong jaw.

Warmth spread through me as I watched him. I wanted him now even more than I had that first night when he was just some hot, nameless guy at a bar. Now, he was so much more than that.

He stood up and glanced over at me. When our eyes

met, a warm shiver raced through me. What was it about this man that tore down all my defenses?

Hoping to get my mind off all the sudden emotion I was feeling, I suggested we ride the little train that drove throughout the zoo. Maddie got a kick out of holding up her arms like she was on a roller coaster, and by the end of the train ride, my face hurt from laughing so much.

By the time we'd finished at the zoo, it was almost closing time.

"I'm starving," Maddie declared as we walked toward the car.

"If you guys are up for it, I know of some good dinner spots around here. My treat," I said as Hunter buckled Maddie into the backseat.

"You've already done enough, Kate," Hunter said as he settled into the front seat.

"I want to." I smiled. "Besides, I need to continue your culinary education."

He gave me a crooked grin. "Well, if it's going to be educational, I can't really say no, can I?"

I directed him to take us to one of my favorite vegan restaurants. It was hard to please kids, especially with health food, but I had a feeling Maddie would appreciate it. Especially because I knew they had an extensive gluten-free menu.

Once we were seated at our table, I raised my water glass. "Cheers to a great day."

"It was awesome," Maddie said as we clinked glasses. She picked up her menu, holding it upside down.

I turned the menu around and read her some of the options, sensing Hunter's gaze on me as I helped Maddie settle on a gluten-free mac and cheese. When the food arrived, Hunter and Maddie dove into their meals excitedly.

"This is actually good," Hunter said, surprise in his voice as he took another bite of his sandwich.

Maddie seemed equally impressed.

We finished off our meal by splitting a vegan cupcake. A pang of sadness hit me as we left the restaurant; I wasn't ready for the night to end, but I didn't think I could continue to hold them hostage any longer.

When we pulled up to the house, Maddie jumped out of the car and started to run inside.

"Maddie, what do you have to say to Kate?" Hunter asked before she'd gone inside.

She stopped in her tracks, turning back to me, then ran over and gave me another hug. "Thank you," she said, her head resting on my stomach.

"Anytime." I patted her on the head, my heart swelling.

After she'd gone inside, Hunter walked me over to my door.

"Thanks for today. We had a great time." He smiled at me, making my insides warm again. "I have a feeling Maddie is going to be talking about today for a while."

I leaned against the door frame. His lips looked so good that it took all my restraint not to kiss him.

"I had a great time too." I smiled, purposely lingering.

I wondered if I should tell him how I'd been feeling, just blurt it out and get it out in the open, but I couldn't come up with the words. It was such a perfect moment; all I had to do was say it.

God, I was so terrible at this. No wonder I'd never had a relationship. I needed to figure out the right way to tell him how I felt before I totally lost my mind.

"Well, good night," I finally said, unable to handle the silence any longer.

"Good night."

His gaze on mine seemed so heavy, almost magnetic, like I couldn't look away. I felt like he was waiting for me to say something, but my heart was pounding so hard, I didn't think I could get any words out. I quickly stepped inside and smiled at him one more time before shutting the door behind me.

As I walked upstairs to my apartment, I sighed. That wasn't my smoothest moment. He'd probably been waiting for me to make the first move, and instead I'd messed it up by being totally awkward.

As I walked by the window, I noticed the light on in Hunter's room. I felt another twinge of sadness that I wasn't going home with him and Maddie. The day had been so fun and comfortable; it had almost been like we were a real family.

I hoped he'd understood what I was trying to tell him by planning the day, but I knew I needed to work up the courage to tell him how I felt before I lost him.

Chapter Eighteen

Hunter

Today had been entirely unexpected. I would have never imagined that Kate of all people could plan such a kid-friendly date. Watching her excitement when we strolled into the zoo and seeing Maddie light up at the baby foxes—it had honestly been one of the best days in a long time.

Maybe that was crazy of me to think, but it was true. Until Kate came into our lives, I hadn't realized quite how hungry I was for a real relationship with a woman.

Of course, it was with the same woman who had sat me down prior to our first hookup and made me promise that we'd keep this casual and had talked about avoiding developing feelings like it was a fatal disease. God, how badly I wished that she wanted the same things I did.

After the day we'd had, it didn't surprise me at all how quickly Maddie went to sleep. As I crept out of her room, closing the door gently behind me, I grabbed the monitor I rarely used, planning to walk over to Kate's place to thank her one more time and say good night.

Today had gone so smoothly, even after I admitted my feelings to her at the park the other day. I was worried that what I said might have scared her off, but after the day we had, it felt like maybe she'd just let that indiscretion go.

I knocked on Kate's door, and within moments, she opened it, a small smile on her face. Even though we'd spent the whole day together, I couldn't help but be a little blown away by her beauty. Her hair was swept back into a loose braid, and she'd changed into a pair of yoga pants and a soft-looking T-shirt. Even in casual loungewear, she was sexy. And the way she was looking at me, with that sweet little smile and that knowing look in her eye? My heart thumped fast.

"Is Maddie asleep?" she asked, stepping aside to let me in.

I held up the monitor. "I could barely keep her awake long enough to brush her teeth."

Even though I'd been to Kate's apartment a dozen times by now, seeing what she'd done with the place still brought a smile to my face. When I'd listed this little apartment above my garage, I'd imagined some sad loner moving into it, someone who would barely be a blip on my radar except once a month to pay rent and utilities. But Kate had breathed new life into what used to be an empty, unused space. Part of me wondered if I was still talking about the apartment, or my heart.

From her pristine kitchen tools to her killer record collection, to her smile and sex appeal, Kate was a total and complete surprise to me. Honestly, I couldn't imagine my life without her.

"Can I get you something to drink? Water? Wine? I picked up a new bottle of red a couple days ago that I think might actually be decent, even though it was only six dollars." She walked into her kitchen and pulled out a dark bottle with a white label on it, holding it up to read the description.

"A glass of wine would be great."

I followed her into the kitchen and took a seat at the table. She set the bottle on the counter and pulled a wine opener out of one of the drawers.

"Need any help getting that bottle open?" I asked.

"The day I need a man to open my wine for me is the day I give up drinking." She scoffed, popping the cork out of the bottle with ease. "I appreciate you asking, though," she added with a grin.

After taking a couple of stemless wineglasses down from the shelf, Kate poured us each a glass and joined me at the table. I thanked her and took the glass in my hand, very aware of our fingers brushing with the exchange.

"To independent women," I said, raising my glass into the air.

Kate smiled, arching a playful eyebrow and cocking her head to the side. "And to the men who are secure enough to let them stay that way," she said, clinking her glass to mine.

I smiled back and took a sip of the wine while Kate did the same. It was sweeter than I expected and didn't exactly taste like wine, but it was still drinkable.

"Grape juice. That tastes exactly like grape juice," Kate said, shaking her head and swirling the liquid around in her glass.

"Nothing wrong with a six-dollar bottle of grape juice," I replied, giving her a reassuring smile.

Kate shrugged and took another sip of wine.

"So, uh, hey, I just wanted to say thank you for today," I said, trying to get my thoughts in order before I completely scared her off for good. "Maddie's mom isn't around, and the older she gets, the more I worry about her having good female figures in her life. So, spending all this time with you, especially today . . . it means a lot. I know you're not really into the whole kid thing—which I completely understand—but still, you were a natural."

Kate stared at me, her eyes wide and her brows raised. Then she chuckled softly, looking down at her hands and shaking her head. "That's what I wanted to show you today. I didn't want to just tell you with words, I wanted you to see what I want, how I feel about Maddie . . . and you."

She looked up at me then, her eyes meeting mine with a tenderness I had rarely seen from her before.

"I've fallen for you," Kate said, her eyes still locked with mine. "Both of you. I know you're a package deal, and that's what I want. I didn't think I wanted this in my future; I always thought being tied down would feel like, well, being tied down. I had no idea how good it could feel—like I've finally found my people, the tribe that I belong to."

My throat was thick with emotion, but Kate wasn't done.

"Once I met you and saw how my future could look, it all became so clear. I want more."

I reached out and took her hands in mine, running my thumbs over her knuckles. "You have no idea how good it feels to hear you say that." I brought her fingers to my lips, letting the reality of Kate's words sink in. This was everything I ever wanted.

"Come on," I said, still holding her hand as I rose from my seat.

"Where are we—"

She stood and started to speak, but before she could finish her sentence, I pulled her to me and pressed my lips to hers. She sighed, her body softening against mine as she wrapped her arms around me. One slow kiss became three or four quicker ones.

"Let's go," I said, suddenly pulling away and leading Kate to the front door. She nodded and followed, her mouth still slightly open as we made our way to my house.

Once inside, the two of us crept up the stairs and quietly past Maddie's room to mine. Kate and I might have been on the same page, but I hadn't talked to Maddie about any of this yet, and the last thing we needed was to freak her out again.

When we reached my bedroom, I ushered Kate in, pulling the door closed and making sure—as always—to lock it behind us.

I turned around to find her sitting on the edge of my bed. Our eyes locked and she reached her hand out toward me, turning it over and curling her index finger toward her in a come-hither motion. My cock stirred in my pants as I walked toward her, my mind swimming with all the things I wanted to do to her.

It was a powerful thing knowing she felt the same way about me that I did about her.

I joined her on the bed, propping myself over her

body. Our mouths met with a newfound urgency, our bodies instinctively moving against each other. She ran her hands over my back and up to my neck, curling her fingers through my hair. I trailed my lips down to the tender skin at the crook of her neck, and Kate moaned softly. My cock stirred again at the sounds she was making, and suddenly I hated the fact that we both still had our clothes on.

Sitting up, I pulled Kate with me, taking the hem of her T-shirt between my fingers. She raised her arms above her head as I pulled the soft fabric over her body, revealing a lacy light-pink bra underneath. I couldn't help the low growl the sight of her perfect breasts brought out of me.

She grinned, pulling my shirt over my head as well. She wrapped her arms around my neck as we kissed again, and I reached out to unfasten her bra from behind. Within seconds, I had the clasp undone, and both of us sighed as she pressed her breasts against my bare skin.

Perfection. She was sheer perfection.

My tongue swirled against hers and I took her breast in my hand, massaging it gently and pinching her nipple between my fingers. Kate moaned softly, moving her hand up my thigh to the growing erection in my pants.

I groaned at the feel of her fingers over my cock, and quickly grew frustrated by the fabric between them. As Kate continued rubbing my rock-hard manhood, I slipped my fingers under the waistband of her leggings, reaching down to touch her wet panties.

She gasped as my fingers met her damp skin.

After a few moments, I needed more, and I pulled my hand out of Kate's pants, causing her to whimper softly. Peeling the leggings away from her, I ran my tongue down her thigh as I lowered them inch by inch, nibbling gently on her soft skin. Once her leggings were off, I tugged her panties off too, tossing them onto the floor. In one swift motion, I removed my own pants and underwear, my cock springing free and aching to be inside her.

Kate lay on her back and opened her legs to invite me closer. I lowered myself over her, aligning myself at the needy spot between her legs.

"I want you inside me," she whispered, shifting her

hips to tease my tip.

"Condom?" I asked.

She shook her head. "I'm on birth control. And I trust you."

Locking my eyes with hers, I entered her, slowly burying my shaft into her, inch by inch. When I was completely inside, Kate sighed and closed her eyes, reveling in the pleasure of being completely filled.

I brought my lips to hers as I pumped my hips, slowly and gently at first, our kisses tender and sweet. Kate rocked her hips in time with my movements, and as we established a rhythm, each of us groaned with pleasure.

When I felt her tightening around me and sensed she was getting close, I reached down to rub my thumb over her slick bud, a move that always drove her crazy. The moment I applied pressure there, she threw her head back with a gasp that quickly turned into a moan.

Watching her take her pleasure and hearing the sounds she made turned me on to no end, causing my balls to tighten and pressure to build low in my spine. Just as she began to let go, her body constricting around mine, I followed her over the edge, waves of pleasure dragging both of us under at the same time.

Once the waves subsided, I rolled over and onto my back next to Kate, both of us panting.

"That . . . was . . . incredible," she said between breaths, running her hand over my chest.

"You're amazing." I stroked every inch of silky skin I could find—her shoulders, the curve of her hip, her thigh.

Kate rolled onto her side and propped her head on her elbow, a new sparkle in her eye. "A pretty good end to a pretty good day, don't you think?"

"Absolutely." I leaned over and kissed the back of her hand.

She smiled, then leaned into me and placed a long, deep kiss on my lips. "I'll be right back," she said, rising and walking to the bathroom.

As Kate cleaned up, I lay in bed and stared at the ceiling, one arm behind my head. I still couldn't believe she actually wanted more, after everything she'd sworn she'd never want. It seemed almost too good to be true.

I rolled onto my side and saw my cell phone on the bedside table. A thought hit me, and my stomach sank.

There was still the matter of talking to Maddie. While she seemed to really like Kate, and I obviously really appreciated Kate's presence in her life, the last thing I wanted was for Maddie to feel blindsided. My daughter and I had never really talked about what would happen if I was in a relationship, and the more I thought about it, the more worried I became about how she would take it.

Kate returned from the bathroom and crawled into bed next to me, curling her body next to mine. "Whatcha thinking about?" she asked, brushing her fingers across my jaw.

"Nothing," I said, still staring at the ceiling. When Kate didn't respond, I could feel her staring at me and knew I'd have to give her something. "Actually, I just remembered. We should probably set an alarm for the morning, so we can get up and moving before Maddie does."

Kate pulled her hand away from my hair. I turned to

look at her and was surprised to see a hurt look on her face. She knew I was a dad, that I had obligations. Then she gave me a tight-lipped smile and nodded.

"We'll talk about it more in the morning." I placed a soft kiss on her forehead before rolling over to pick up my phone. I set an alarm for five thirty, my mind still buzzing with worry about how this new future would play out.

Chapter Nineteen

Kate

I stared out the window, lost in thought. I still couldn't believe I'd told Hunter how I felt and that he felt the same. It had been less than twenty-four hours ago, and I was still reeling from the experience. It was so picture perfect that I was having a hard time convincing myself that it wasn't all too good to be true.

And yet, a sliver of doubt nagged at me. When he'd set the alarm for me to sneak out this morning, I'd been hurt, but I tried to reason with myself that he just didn't want Maddie finding out that way. It would probably bring up traumatic memories for her to see me coming out of Hunter's room in the morning, and I got that. But I couldn't help wondering if his doing that meant something else entirely. Was he not sure about starting a relationship? Or did he not see a long-term future for us?

I knew I was being childish, but I couldn't help it. Apparently, this was what having feelings for someone did to you—it made you totally irrational. I was determined not to let my overactive imagination get me down, especially because Hunter had texted me earlier asking me to come over. I assumed he wanted to discuss what I'd told him last night, but he hadn't given any hints as to what exactly he had to say about it.

I sprayed perfume on my wrists and rubbed them together. I was trying to stay calm, but in truth, I was a nervous wreck. I'd never put myself out there the way I had yesterday, and I was terrified of being rejected, or that somehow it would all go wrong.

I brushed my teeth and headed down the stairs, sending myself positive energy. I rang his doorbell, fluffing my hair as I waited for him to answer it.

When Hunter pulled open the door, my heart jumped into my throat at the sight of him. Even after everything that had happened, I was still blown away by how attractive he was. And not just his smoking-hot body and killer smile, but by the little happy dance I did inside whenever I was around him.

"Hey, come on in." He gestured me inside, and I followed him.

"Where's Maddie?" I asked as I stepped into the living room, expecting to see her there.

"She went to a friend's house for a birthday party," he said, leading me over to the couch.

I settled in, smoothing my skirt anxiously as he sat next to me. As nervous as I was, I still found myself distracted by being near Hunter. He'd shaven recently, making his chiseled jawline even more prominent, and the scent of aftershave hung in the air between us. I could just make out the definition of his biceps underneath his T-shirt, and on the walk to the couch, I'd gotten a glimpse of how good his butt looked in his black jeans.

He smiled, and I wanted to kiss him right then. But I didn't.

Talking first.

"So," he said, rubbing the back of his neck. "Last night . . ."

When he trailed off for a moment, my heart sank. Then he took a deep breath and continued.

"I just wanted us to get on the same page about what

we're expecting from this. I really like you. I liked you from the beginning, but I knew you didn't want to be involved in something serious. So, I guess I'm just wondering if you meant everything you said last night."

I scooted closer to him on the couch. My thoughts and emotions were running a mile a minute, but I was starting to feel my anxiety melt away. He wanted this to be serious as much as I did.

"Of course I meant it," I said, putting a hand on top of his to assure him. "I'm ready for this. I want to be here for you. And for Maddie. I know I've always said I didn't want a relationship, but it was just because I was afraid. And I obviously hadn't found the right person."

A smile broke out on his face and he put his arm around me, running his fingers along my shoulder.

His eyes met mine, and a delighted quiver ran through me. "If we do this, I want it all."

My heart pumped faster. "Everything. It's yours."

I was ready to leave behind all my fears and doubts, and be in a committed relationship with Hunter—and with Maddie. And now that we were here in this moment, my worries almost seemed ridiculous. What had I been so afraid of? Being with Hunter was the easiest thing in the world.

He leaned in to kiss me, his full lips pressing against mine.

After a few more sweet kisses, I pulled back. "If we're going to do this, I want to do it right. Before we go any further, I think we need to tell Maddie." She had warmed up to me more than I'd expected lately, so I hoped it would go smoothly.

"Yeah, I guess we do." He sighed, worry etched on his face.

I raised an eyebrow at him. "Hunter, are you afraid of your own daughter?"

"What can I say? She's intimidating." He grinned, then reached out to brush my hair behind my ear. "But seriously, no matter how she reacts when we tell her, it'll be okay. She'll get used to it. Besides, she really does like you. I hope you understand my anxiety; it's just been me and her all these years."

He pulled me toward him so that my head was

resting on his chest. My heart swelled as I looked up at him.

"I know, Hunter. Don't worry; everything will work out."

I sighed, allowing myself to melt into his arms. For everyone's sake, I hoped he was right.

•••

"Maddie, dinner is here," Hunter called to her out the back door. She'd been dropped off by a friend's mom just in time for dinner. We'd ordered in from her favorite Mexican restaurant, plus I'd gone out to stock up on ingredients for hot fudge sundaes. We figured if we fed her enough good food, she'd be more likely to support our relationship.

She ran in, and her face lit up when she saw the spread. "Why'd you get this?" she asked, her happy smile turning to a suspicious stare.

"We just wanted to do something special." Hunter grinned, ruffling her hair.

If she was still suspicious, she kept it quiet. I piled

her plate with taco meat, beans, and rice.

"How was the party, Maddie?" I asked as we settled in to eat. I figured we'd sedate her with the food first, then bring up the change in our relationship—from landlord and tenant to boyfriend and girlfriend.

"I jumped on a trampoline," she said excitedly after she swallowed a mouthful of rice.

"That's impressive." I smiled at her. "I was afraid of trampolines until I was six."

"I'm not afraid of anything," Maddie said proudly.

I snorted. "You know what? I believe you."

Soon, we'd finished dinner, and I started setting up the sundae bar.

"So, we've got chocolate and vanilla ice cream, sprinkles, fudge, peanuts, and cherries." I showed her the different options I'd laid out.

"Awesome." She grinned, standing on tiptoe to get a better look.

"Which toppings do you want?" Hunter asked,

scooping out vanilla into a bowl for Maddie.

"I want Kate to make it," she said, glancing over at me.

Hunter laughed, putting his hands up. "I guess she doesn't trust my cooking anymore now that you've come around," he said, handing the bowl to me.

I couldn't believe how great it felt to be with them like this, and I hoped Maddie felt the same.

"Fudge and sprinkles?" I asked Maddie, and she nodded enthusiastically.

Once we'd all sat down with our ice cream, Hunter and I made eye contact. Now was the perfect time to tell her. I took a deep breath, mentally preparing myself for the worst-case scenario.

"So, Maddie, we have something to tell you," Hunter began gently.

She paused with her spoon halfway to her mouth, ice cream dripping over the sides. "What?" she asked, setting the spoon down.

"Well, Kate and I have been spending a lot of time

together . . ."

I tried to keep the smile plastered on my face, but really, I just wanted him to spit it out. Patience really wasn't my strong suit.

Luckily, he continued quickly. "We really like each other, and we're in a relationship now. So you'll be seeing even more of her around here."

There was a beat of silence.

"That's it?" Maddie asked, picking up the spoon again and taking a bite. "Duh. I knew that." She paused. "I think it's cool."

Hunter and I exchanged glances, then burst out laughing.

"What?" Maddie gave us both a perplexed look. "You guys are so weird."

Grinning stupidly to keep from laughing, I dipped my spoon into my sundae and took a bite. Things might have started off unconventionally, but I had a feeling we were headed for a very happy ending.

Chapter Twenty

Hunter

Six months later

The smell of ginger and spices wafted through the air as I walked through the front door, a plastic bag of groceries hanging from my hand. The door swung shut behind me, and I entered the kitchen to find Kate and Maddie huddled around the table, laser-focused on constructing an epic gluten-free gingerbread house.

"How are my girls?" I asked, setting the bag of sweets on the table and leaning down to place a kiss on top of Maddie's head.

"Did you remember to get the little red dots?" Maddie asked, looking at me like her question was the most serious thing she'd ever asked me and that my life depended on the answer.

"Yes, ma'am," I replied, stepping around the table to kiss Kate hello. "I got a little something for you too," I added.

"Aw, thanks, babe," Kate said, barely looking up from her task. She was squeezing a huge tube of white frosting, meticulously dispensing the sugary glue between two slabs of gingerbread.

Once she finished piping the frosting, she set the tube down on the table and gently pressed the two edges together. "Okay, Maddie, now we just need to wait for this last wall to dry, and then it'll be time to really get our decorating on."

Maddie nodded silently, her eyes trained on the newly laid frosting.

"How about some hot chocolate while we wait?" I offered, unpacking the candies from the bag.

"Yay!" Maddie quickly clambered down from her chair at the table and scurried to the pantry to help me get the hot chocolate ingredients.

Once Maddie was out of earshot, I placed a hand on Kate's shoulder and asked, "How was she while I was gone? She's listening to you, right? No issues?"

Kate chuckled and shook her head. "Just because I've moved in doesn't mean that things are going to change between Maddie and me. She was perfect. You really don't need to worry about us."

I let out a sigh of relief. Kate had moved in for good last week. I'd figured there might be an adjustment period for all three of us, but so far, things had gone smoothly. "I know you're right. I just worry sometimes, you know? This is still new territory for all of us."

"Well, I appreciate your concern, but trust me, everything's perfect." Kate smiled, and I leaned down to kiss her again, this time a little longer than before.

"Daddy!" Maddie called out. "Come help me make hot chocolate!"

I broke away from the kiss, and Kate let out a small giggle.

"I guess that's something we'll just have to get used to, won't we?"

"You'd think we'd be used to being interrupted by now," I said with a wink. We both laughed, and I walked over to the fridge and pulled out the milk.

"Hey, Daddy?"

"Yeah, Maddie?"

"Is Kate gonna live with us forever?"

Shit. When Kate and I decided she should move in, we'd had a talk with Maddie about it, but she didn't have many questions at the time. Kate had said she thought that was a good sign, but I'd been worried. And now that Maddie was asking me questions like that? I wasn't sure what her reaction would be, no matter how I responded.

"That's the plan," I said, turning the heat to low and setting the wooden spoon on the counter. "Is that okay with you? I know we talked about it before and you said it was okay, but it's also okay if you're scared about it now."

Maddie shook her head, looking down at her toes. "No, I'm not scared," she said, picking at a piece of frosting stuck to her shirt.

"Then what is it, sweetie?"

"I just really like it that she lives here now."

I smiled, crouching down and pulling Maddie in for a hug. "Me too."

I gave the hot chocolate one final stir before taking

three mugs out of the cabinet. As I poured the hot liquid into the mugs, Maddie followed closely behind, dropping a handful of mini marshmallows into each one.

"Do you want a candy cane in yours?" I asked, ripping the bag open and pulling out one of the mini red-and-white candies.

Maddie shook her head vigorously. "No, that's gross."

"Well, I want one." I hooked a candy cane over the lip of the mug. "Kate, do you want a candy cane in your hot chocolate?" I called over to her.

"No, that's gross," she called back.

Maddie and I both laughed.

"See? I told you." Maddie raised her eyebrows and placed her hands on her hips.

Maybe I wasn't as prepared for this whole two-against-one thing as I thought. It was hard enough with one XX gender in the house, let alone two. I was seriously outnumbered.

I carried Kate and Maddie's mugs over to the table

while Maddie climbed into the chair next to Kate, sitting up on her knees to get a better view of the house.

"Is it ready?" Maddie asked.

"Just about." Kate smiled. "In the meantime, why don't we start opening these bags of candy."

"I'll get you some bowls," I said. As I walked across the kitchen toward the cabinet, Maddie and Kate continued chattering behind me, their giggles and laughter bringing a huge smile to my face.

Kate and Maddie got to work on decorating the house, Maddie pointing out the places she wanted to put a gumdrop, and Kate piping a small dot of frosting in the exact spot. They were a great team. Kate was patient with Maddie when she continually changed her mind at the last second, and Maddie hung on Kate's every word. It was sweet. I really couldn't have picked a better woman for my daughter to look up to. Kate was strong, confident, and independent, all the things I wanted Maddie to be.

By the time they were making their finishing touches about half an hour later, the gingerbread house looked perfect—and the two of them were completely covered in frosting and sugar.

"What do you think, Daddy?" Maddie asked when they were done, proudly outstretching her arms around their creation.

"You two did a great job."

She smiled, staring at the gingerbread house with pride. Suddenly, her gaze snapped over to Kate.

"When do we get to eat it?"

•••

A couple of hours later, we put Maddie to bed and headed into our bedroom. I made sure to close our door, but I didn't need to lock it anymore. Maddie knew to knock if she needed anything.

While I changed, Kate stood in the bathroom, washing the final bits of frosting off her hands.

"I don't know if I'll ever get this sugar out from underneath my fingernails," she said, pulling a nailbrush out of the drawer and scrubbing at her fingertips.

"That just means you'll be even sweeter than you

already are," I replied, tossing my jeans into the hamper and pulling my T-shirt off over my head.

Kate snorted. "That's super corny, babe."

"Dad jokes come with the territory." I shrugged. "Having second thoughts about moving in?"

She smiled, her gaze wandering lazily over my bare chest. She walked over to me and ran her hands over my biceps before wrapping her arms around my neck. "Not even a little."

I pulled her close, tipping her chin up to meet mine, and took her lips in a sweet kiss. My cock gave an eager twitch in my boxers. And judging by the look on Kate's face, she felt it too.

She arched an eyebrow, pressing her body a little harder into mine. "How you doing there, big guy?"

I let my hands wander down her back to her perfect ass, taking a handful of her cheeks in each hand and squeezing, causing her to arch her back, rubbing her body against mine.

"I think you know how I'm doing." I growled,

bringing my lips to her neck, grazing the tender spot below her ear.

She sighed, leaning her head back and running her fingers through my hair.

"Why don't you show me?" she said breathlessly, trailing her fingernails over my back, sending desire shooting straight up my spine.

I growled again into her neck, my cock now straining against my boxers and pressing into her belly.

Releasing her ass, I pulled her top over her head, quickly undoing the clasp on her bra to reveal her full, supple breasts. Taking one of her nipples in my mouth, I sucked on it gently and Kate moaned, running her fingers through my hair again.

As I continued kissing and sucking on her breast, I moved my hands to the waist of her jeans, unbuttoning them and pulling the zipper down.

Leading her to our bed, I pulled Kate on top of me, her legs straddling my hips. Taking my cock in her delicate hands, she guided me as she lowered herself, taking me inch by inch, both of us moaning as she did. Once I was fully inside her, Kate leaned down, bringing her lips to mine, and for a moment neither one of us moved, relishing how amazing it felt to be one.

When our lips parted, I placed my hand on her cheek, my eyes searching hers.

"There's something I want to tell you," I whispered, running my thumb over her skin.

"What is it?" she whispered back, turning her face to place a small kiss on my palm.

I paused, taking in her beauty for what felt like the first time all over again. Her hair, her eyes, her full, pouty lips . . . she was everything. I never thought I would find someone who could handle Maddie and me as a package deal, and somehow, I tricked the universe into giving Kate to me. I couldn't believe how lucky I was, and I couldn't keep my feelings to myself anymore.

"I love you," I said, staring deeply into her eyes. "And I want to keep you forever."

Her eyes widened for a moment, then glistened with unshed tears. She was silent for a few seconds more before letting out a soft chuckle.

“I love you too,” she replied, smiling and wiping the corner of her eye. “But forever’s a long time. Are you sure?”

“Forever won’t be nearly long enough.” I pulled her in for another kiss, the energy between us suddenly electric. Our mouths moved quickly and urgently against each other as our bodies found a pleasurable rhythm.

Kate rocked her hips over me, sending immediate waves of pleasure through my whole body.

“Yes, that’s it. Like that.” I groaned, placing one hand on her ass to guide her movements, and brought the other between her legs to rub her clit.

Her moans grew louder as mine grew deeper, and our breathing became ragged. As Kate came closer to orgasm, her eyes never left mine. God, I could have watched her all night like this, the pleasure on her face all my doing.

Forever definitely wouldn’t be nearly long enough.

Chapter Twenty-One

Kate

I never thought I'd be the type to want a big, fluffy white dress. First, there was the expense, and second, it was just so damn impractical. Third, it was uncomfortable and obnoxious, and something you only wore once. It seemed like a complete waste.

Yet when the time came to plan our big day, a newfound part of me I'd never been acquainted with began voicing her opinions. I'd told Hunter this would be a low-key affair—a simple backyard barbecue, for all I cared. But the further we got in the planning, the more specific my requests became.

Suddenly, the backyard wasn't quite enough, yet a banquet hall was too sterile; a pantsuit was something you wore to a funeral, and a sundress was too casual. He'd been sweet and accommodating of my every whim, which was how we came to be sitting in the private back room of our favorite restaurant, me in a stunning white gown that cost as much as my first car. There was a small parquet floor for dancing, and about fifty of our closest friends and family gathered around us.

And as for the white dress—you only live once, folks. In this moment, I felt like a princess, and not in a cheesy *I've conformed* kind of way, but in a *bursting with happiness, I've finally found my Prince Charming* kind of way.

I gazed across the room and saw Maddie digging through the gift bag I'd left for her, chatting happily with Hunter's parents and my mom.

The day had been perfect. Our ceremony was short and sweet, and now soft jazz music floated through the air as waiters circled with glasses of bubbly champagne on little silver trays. I couldn't help the smile overtaking my lips.

As Jessie and Rebecca rose to their feet and moved to the front of the room, I could already smell trouble. Jessie had that familiar grin I'd come to recognize meant mischief, and Rebecca swayed next to her, already pleasantly buzzed on champagne.

Dread filled me. What were they going to say? This was supposed to be a family-friendly event.

Jessie tapped a spoon against a glass, drawing everyone's attention.

Hunter's gaze met mine, and he was smiling. God, this man. He looked so freaking happy, so full of life. His eyes were bright, his hair styled so neatly, and his black suit fit him perfectly. I didn't think I'd ever get used to how handsome he was.

"If we could have your attention, please," Jessie said. "We'd like to say a few words to the bride and groom."

The crowd quieted, and all eyes were on Jessie as she straightened her shoulders, thrusting her chin out.

"First, we have to give huge props to Hunter." She looked right at him as she spoke, and Rebecca grinned conspiratorially. "For taming our commitment-phobe friend. She was only looking for Mister Tonight, and we're so happy that she found her Mister Forever."

The collective *aww* from the crowd only marginally soothed my hot shame. There's nothing like your in-laws knowing you once enjoyed lots of no-strings sex.

"Cheers to Kate and Hunter!" Rebecca said, and applause broke out.

Hunter's hand found mine under the table, and he squeezed. "Any second thoughts?"

"Not a one," I said, meaning every word. I wouldn't let Jessie and Rebecca's toast embarrass me. I had been afraid of commitment. But Hunter had changed all that.

"Love you, baby," he murmured, leaning close.

"Love you more."

Soon, appetizers were delivered to the tables and my friends took their seats once again. Later there would be dinner and dancing, and then a special night away at a hotel suite for Hunter and me while Maddie stayed over with her grandparents. And next month, we'd take our honeymoon—a seven-night trip to Scotland that I'd been dreaming about for months.

But it wasn't the dress, or the party, or the honeymoon I was most excited about. It was a lifetime of being Hunter's wife and Maddie's mom that had my heart near bursting.

"Daddy!" Maddie came bounding over to the table where Hunter and I sat huddled together. "Look at what I got!" She held up the loot from her gift bag. "It's a princess coloring book."

Hunter nodded, patting her shoulder. "Kate picked all that out for you."

Her bright gaze swung over to me. "Thanks, Kate!"

"You're very welcome. I wanted to make sure you have fun tonight too."

Hunter smiled, watching our interaction. "And later when you're tired, Grandma and Grandpa will take you home, okay?"

"I'm not tired," Maddie insisted. "I want to dance."

Hunter and I chuckled as we watched her sashay around in her frilly party dress.

"Kate?" Maddie asked, her expression suddenly turning serious. "Since you're married to my daddy now, does that mean you're my mommy?"

My stomach twisted as I glanced at Hunter, hoping for some help. But he only grinned. "Um, well, I would love to be your mommy. I didn't grow you in my belly, but I love you very much, and I—"

"Okay, good," Maddie said quickly. "So I can start calling you Mommy now?"

My throat tightened as tears gathered in my eyes. "Would you want to?"

"Yup!" Maddie cheered.

I pulled her little body close, wrapping her in a hug, and could swear my heart swelled three sizes. "I would love that."

After that, she scampered away, leaving Hunter and me to stare at each other with unshed tears. He placed his hand on my cheek, watching me with so much emotion in his eyes.

It had taken me a long time to learn what a four-year-old already knew. A mom was someone who took you to the zoo and kissed your boo-boos and made you chocolate chip cookies. Someone who spent every day making sure you were happy and loved.

Maddie was right. I was her mom now.

I beamed at Hunter, unable to hide my smile. "That was incredible."

He nodded. "You were made for this role." His warm gaze stayed glued to mine, seeming to calm me and communicate *you've got this* all at once.

I pressed a quick kiss to his lips.

"Mister Tonight, huh?" he asked, recalling Jessie's words.

I rolled my eyes. "Obviously, that didn't work out."

"I'd say it worked out perfectly."

Against the backdrop of silverware clinking against glassware, I pressed my lips to Hunter's again.

Epilogue

Kate

"A little to the left," I told Hunter, shifting my hips. "Right there! That's perfect."

He adjusted himself and continued stroking my inner thigh. "I just want you to be comfortable, baby."

Even after being married for almost a year, we were still as hot and heavy as ever. And it didn't hurt that I was nine months pregnant and my hormones were giving me the libido of a teenage boy. The problem was, we couldn't always find a position that worked for my gigantic belly. And did I mention I was having twins?

Hunter moved his hand lower and stroked exactly where I wanted him. "You're so wet, baby," he whispered as I let out a moan. He moved forward, ready to position his erection up against me, when I felt a sharp stab of pain in my abdomen.

I gasped, clutching my stomach.

"What is it?" he asked, concern lacing his voice. "Is it

the babies?"

The pain subsided, and I let out a sigh of relief.

"It's fine, just keep going," I told him.

It had taken us fifteen minutes to figure out the perfect position, and I'd be damned if I gave up on an orgasm now. Hunter didn't seem convinced, so I placed a hand on his thick erection, moving my hand up and down. I shifted my hips forward, ready for him to enter me, when I was hit with another wave.

"Shit," I whispered, the wind knocked out of me from the pain.

"I think we should go to the hospital," he said, jumping up and beginning to pull his clothes on.

"I'm not due until next week," I protested, shaking my head.

He placed his hand on my cheek, tucking my hair behind my ear. "Come on, I think we should get this checked out. I don't want you in pain."

"No, I'm fine. I think it's a false alarm," I said, waving him away. "I'm just going to rest for a little."

Hunter was unconvinced. Ignoring me, he pulled my overnight bag out from the closet and picked up my clothes from the floor.

"You need to put these on," he said, placing my feet through my panties and pulling them up for me. Then he grabbed his cell. His parents had agreed to watch Maddie while we were at the hospital, and were waiting on standby.

Reluctantly, I pulled on the rest of my clothes before sitting on the bed while Hunter spoke to his mother. When he hung up, he grabbed the suitcase.

"I'm going to load the car while they drive over," he said, leaning over to press a kiss to the top of my head.

Throughout the pregnancy, Hunter had been a bundle of nerves. Anytime I walked too fast or tripped on the sidewalk (which, unfortunately, I did a lot), he'd run over to me to make sure that the babies and I were okay. I would have thought he'd be the levelheaded one since he'd been through this before. I, on the other hand, had been surprisingly calm for the past nine months, other than my raging hormones and intense cravings for chocolate and pickles.

But suddenly, I wasn't so sure. I didn't feel ready to bring two lives into this world quite yet.

Was it too late to back out of this whole thing?

We'd found out I was pregnant a couple of months after the wedding. Shortly after, I legally adopted Maddie, and when we told her about her new brothers, we were worried she'd be upset. In typical Maddie fashion, she'd been mature about everything and couldn't wait to meet them. She'd already made a list of activities they could do together once the twins were old enough. And until then, she had a list of things she could do to help us. She reminded us that with two babies around, there wouldn't be as much time for the two of us to have adult snuggle-time, so she'd watch her brothers so we could still do that.

Hunter ran back up the stairs. Winded, he helped me stand up.

"Let's get you in the car now so we can be ready." He took a deep inhale. "They should be here any minute."

I bit my lip, not moving.

"Kate?" he asked, finally pausing for a moment to give me a long look. "Is it the contractions? Does it hurt too much to walk?"

I shook my head, not looking at him.

"What is it?" He came to stand next to me and put an arm around me.

"I watched a lot of reality TV," I blurted, feeling tears well up.

"What are you talking about?" he asked, confused.

"You know how you're supposed to play Mozart while you're pregnant so your baby turns out smarter? Well, I didn't. I just watched a lot of reality TV, and now the twins are going to be stupid and it's my fault." I put my head in my hands while Hunter wrapped an arm around me. "I'm already a bad mom."

Okay, I knew I was probably being a little hysterical, but I couldn't stop myself. The reality that I was about to shape two lives was hitting me harder than it ever had before. This was adulting at a whole new level. Was I really ready?

"Hey, they won't be stupid," he said softly, rubbing my shoulder. "They're going to be great. And you're going to be a great mom. You already are, baby. Look how you are with Maddie."

Unconvinced, I nodded. Another contraction hit, and I squeezed Hunter's hand until the pain passed.

"Come on, we have to get going," he said, taking my hand and guiding me to the hall.

"No, I'm not in labor," I said, shaking my head. "I still have a week."

Suddenly, I felt something between my legs. I looked up at Hunter.

"I think my water just broke," I said in disbelief.

He jumped into action, lifting me off my feet and whisking me down the stairs. His parents pulled up just as he was helping me into the car. They waved at us as we pulled away, Hunter's mom already crying with happiness.

I was still in a state of shock as we drove to the hospital. Of course, I was prepared for this moment—we'd gone to all the classes, had read the books we were supposed to read. We'd bought two cribs and a double stroller, and we had a dresser full of tiny, freshly washed baby clothes. Hunter and I had practiced swaddling a fake baby about a thousand times. But now that it was happening, I felt completely unprepared.

We pulled up to the hospital in record time. Hunter wanted to run inside to get me a wheelchair, but I insisted on walking in.

"Seriously, Kate?" he asked as I waddled out of the car.

"I can do it." I huffed, resting one hand on the car for a moment as a contraction shot through me. *Holy hell!*

"Stay here," he told me. "I'm serious. Don't move."

I didn't appreciate being scolded, but I decided to give in. After all, relationships were about letting yourself be supported by another person. It had been a long road, but I'd finally learned that lesson. Sometimes I needed to set my independence aside and let Hunter take the lead.

Everything inside the hospital was such a whirlwind; it felt like only seconds later that I'd been put into a gown and was sitting in a hospital bed. The pain intensified quickly. I didn't consider myself a wimp, but this was seriously no joke. When the pain was almost unbearable, the nurse gave me a sympathetic grin.

"It's almost time to push," she said enthusiastically.

Another wave of pain surged through me. What was she so happy about? I wanted to slap the bitch.

Hunter offered me some ice chips to chew on, which he'd been instructed to do by the nurse. I waved him away.

"I changed my mind about this." I gasped, frantically looking at Hunter. He had a bewildered look on his face, still holding out the ice chips. This was unbearable. What the fuck had I gotten myself into?

"It'll be okay, baby. You can do this," he said, gripping my hand firmly.

"Why did you do this to me?" I groaned.

The doctor strode into the room, along with a couple of nurses who began prepping two bassinets.

My nether regions felt like they were on fire. I looked at Hunter and tried to calm myself by staring into his warm, dark eyes. His expression was full of worry as I gripped his hand with every wave of pain. I tried to tell myself that this would all be a funny story once my lady parts stopped feeling like they were full of hot coals.

A few moments later, my knees were drawn up and I was told to bear down. Whatever the hell that meant.

"You're doing great," Hunter said.

I let out several grunts in response. If I weren't the size of a whale, I would have jumped off the bed and run out of here.

"Just keep looking at me," he told me.

Staring at Hunter was the only thing keeping me grounded, so I kept my eyes locked with his as I continued to push.

After a few more pushes, just when I was about to give up and live as a pregnant woman for the rest of my life, one baby was delivered. Tiny cries filled the room, and I wanted to sob with relief.

"He's perfect," the nurse said excitedly after looking him over.

"One down, one to go," the doctor said, grinning at Hunter.

Fuck.

After another several pushes, the second baby moved into position and was finally free.

Exhausted, I lay back until the nurses brought them over to me, one at a time. I took one look at them and burst into tears. They were so tiny and adorable. My heart was so full, it actually felt close to bursting.

Hunter leaned over and ran a finger along their tiny cheeks. "They're ours," he whispered excitedly.

I tried to control my waterworks, but I couldn't. The babies were too perfect. I couldn't believe I'd ever questioned having a family. This was by far the greatest thing I'd ever experienced.

I watched Hunter as he looked down at our babies, and thought about how amazing it was going to be when Maddie met them.

I'd had a lot of doubts along the way—about dating, marriage, and having a family—but this moment overshadowed every doubt I'd ever had. This was my family, my tribe, my ride-or-die, and it was absolutely perfect.

Bonus Epilogue

Kate

"I think I love them the most when they're sleeping." I peered into the nursery where our six-month-old twins, Simon and Miles, were napping in their cribs. "Is that bad?" I asked Hunter, who stood by my side with his hand at my waist.

"Not at all. You've done amazing, baby. You deserve some rest too."

My lips curled up in a smile. "I love it when you talk dirty to me," I whispered.

Hunter's eyebrows shot up, and he let out a soft chuckle.

I tugged his hand, drawing him past the nursery and into our bedroom. "Telling a sleep-deprived new mother she can nap is practically foreplay."

Smiling, he followed me to the bed, where I promptly collapsed into a comfortable heap, positioning my head on his bicep when he snuggled in beside me.

Maddie was with my mom and Hunter's mom at a photo shoot for a popular boy band that was in town for a concert tonight. I'd pulled a few strings at work and gotten private passes for the event. Maddie had been thrilled.

So far, Hunter and I had a chaotic morning filled with feedings and diaper changes, lullabies and explosive diarrhea—all in all, a typical Saturday. In my previous life, I'd be two mimosas deep right now, and probably chatting with my besties. Instead I was here, raising two tiny humans with the love of my life. Not a bad gig, though I was known to complain sometimes, mostly when I hadn't showered—or slept—in more than two days.

"Close your eyes and rest. If they wake up, I've got it under control."

A lazy smile lingered at my lips as my eyes slipped closed. I enjoyed the feeling of lying next to Hunter, his firm body warming mine.

Without his steady, loving encouragement and all his help, I wouldn't have made it this far. Motherhood was hard, yo. It was easily one of the most rewarding things I'd ever done, but it was also one of the most challenging too.

Thank God my sweet husband kept me grounded.

Maddie had turned out to be an amazing big sister. We'd been prepared for the worst—she'd been an only-child for five years, and we knew it would be normal to feel some jealousy toward the new babies. Yet Maddie had handled it all like a pro.

All in all, life was pretty amazing. We'd named the babies after our favorite musicians from our now commingled vinyl collection, and I'd started working again part-time after four months at home with them. Through it all, Hunter continued to be the supportive, amazing man I first fell in love with. I was one lucky lady, and I knew it.

With a sleepy, satisfied smile on my lips, I closed my eyes letting the blissful feelings lull me into a restful sleep.

Get the Next Book

To ensure you don't miss Kendall Ryan's next book, sign up and you'll get a release-day reminder.

www.kendallryanbooks.com/newsletter

Or Text HOTBOOKS to 22-828

If You Liked *Mister Tonight*, you'll LOVE …

Love Machine by Kendall Ryan

After a rather uncomfortable ladies' night involving a cucumber-wielding instructor with judgy eyes, I'm forced to admit my weaknesses. Rather than point blame at my lack of a sex life, I'm ready to roll up my sleeves and get to work.

As a junior executive who's clawed her way up the corporate ladder, failure is not in my vocabulary. Confident and bold in other areas of my life, I have to admit it's time to up my bedroom game.

Asking my friend Slate Cruz is really the only option. Slate is like a walking billboard for sex. The man gets more ass than a toilet seat. There's no way I'll want more from this playboy than a little inspiration to revive my inner sex kitten.

Except, what happens if I do?

Acknowledgments

Thank you so much to my incredible team, including Danielle Sanchez, who is a publicity and marketing goddess. To Alyssa Garcia, the best executive assistant in the world. What would I do without you? I don't ever want to find out. And to my editing team—Elaine York and Becca Mysoor, a huge amount of gratitude for helping to shape my story; and to Pam Berehulke for your always outstanding edits.

A giant thank-you to all the book bloggers for your tireless efforts to post reviews and participate in blog tours. You guys rock my world. I adore you so much!!

A massive bear hug to all my readers. I am so blessed to get to do this for a living, and I don't take a single one of you for granted. Thank you.

And last, to my husband, John. You believe in me, lift me up, and push me to succeed beyond my wildest dreams. Sometimes superheroes don't wear capes. Mine wears a suit and tie (and often has two babies in his arms.) Love you, babe.

About the Author

A *New York Times*, *Wall Street Journal*, and *USA TODAY* bestselling author of more than two dozen titles, Kendall Ryan has sold over two million books, and her books have been translated into several languages in countries around the world. Her books have also appeared on the *New York Times* and *USA TODAY* bestseller list more than three dozen times. Kendall has been featured in publications such as *USA TODAY*, *Newsweek*, and *In Touch Magazine*. She lives in Texas with her husband and two sons.

Visit Kendall online at: **www.kendallryanbooks.com**

Or on Instagram at:

@kendallryan1

Other Books by Kendall Ryan

Unravel Me

Make Me Yours

Working It

Craving Him

All or Nothing

When I Break Series

Filthy Beautiful Lies Series

The Gentleman Mentor

Sinfully Mine

Bait & Switch

Slow & Steady

The Room Mate

The Play Mate

The House Mate

The Bed Mate

The Soul Mate

Hard to Love

Reckless Love

Resisting Her

The Impact of You

Screwed

Monster Prick

The Fix Up

Sexy Stranger

Dirty Little Secret

Dirty Little Promise

Torrid Little Affair

xo, Zach

Baby Daddy

Tempting Little Tease

Bro Code

For a complete list of Kendall's books, visit:

www.kendallryanbooks.com/all-books/

CPSIA information can be obtained
at www.ICGtesting.com
Printed in the USA
FSHW02n0812140918
52247FS